HER DARK LOVE

DARK SPELL SERIES BOOK 1

ISRA SRAVENHEART

DEDICATION

To the most wondrous of friends that lingered in places amongst waves of imagination and splendour, once upon a time! If only such a friendship had been built to last over time but alas, we cannot focus on the past, can we?

1

On the warmest summer night, sounds could be heard echoing from the forest.

In the midst of the well-kept woods beside some well placed cherry trees was a quaint gray castle where a coven of young witches could be heard chorusing to one another, telling beguiling tales of yet another mysterious and harrowing day that had just ended.

The castle wasn't one you would expect of re-told fabrications from another world. It wasn't a grand palace where you would find queens, kings, and beautiful princesses with long, flowing golden hair! This enchanting establishment housed young witches and warlocks alike, a bountiful place where they could learn and hone in on their most gifted of skills: magic.

This place was owned and managed by a feeble man with silky black hair tumbling down to his neck. He went by the name Magnus Wingdom, and the establishment had been appropriately named Wingdom's Academy of Ancient Magics. It wasn't as much of a school at the moment, as the coven only contained thirteen girls. Yes, *just* girls. It prevented warlocks and witches from getting frisky with each other. That, among many other things, was forbidden!

Young witches would come here to be trained up in their craft, residing in their own coven quarters after the day's learning was done. The school only housed up to a few at a time, but the students could leave whenever they pleased unless they were careless with their craft. Then they would be told to leave as soon as was universally possible. The last thing the coven needed was an embarrassment to their well-groomed establishment!

The winds grew violent as night was just in its beginning. A young witch hurriedly pulled her cloak close to her body, feeling the night's chill upon her skin. She let her hood down gently for a moment to reveal chocolate-brown hair that almost surpassed her back. Her eyes were dominated by that of an emerald green, cleverly blending with the brown hue of her tresses.

Her name was Isra and she was just seventeen. She hadn't long passed her birthday, and now she had come to seek guidance from those who possessed knowledge in the greatest gift of them all. Witchcraft.

Isra had been born a witch. She had known this from her earliest years back when she was able to see those who no longer resided on this earthly plain to more enchanting ideals such as seeing fairies and nature spirits playing in the woods, dazzling her senses as she watched them with vivid curiosity.

She saw worlds beyond any childlike imagination, more than her earthly parents could understand or even encourage. In fact, they did much of the latter. Isra's parents were very grounded, human type people and so she quickly found she did not fit in with their dull world.

It was no trouble to Isra. She knew there had to be something more to this life than one of going to work all day, coming home and arguing with a respective spouse before once again going out to work the next day.

She sought refuge in fantasy, thrilled by entrancing feats where unicorns grazed upon heavenly plains of the greenest grass, delighted by fairies who stared at Isra as she felt gracious to be in their presence. When she felt a need for solitude, she would go down to the ocean where she found mermaids lying across ochre-colored shores, smiling in joy with one another as they combed their hair that glistened brilliantly with the white moonlight.

Alas, Isra was not a child anymore! She couldn't go back to those days even if she wanted to. She was becoming a woman, knowing that life held so many doors for her if only she willed them to open first.

She was here to learn, to excel in her craft. She had already begun basic spells, always having her nose inside the pages of a book, but now she was going to be under the teachings of some of the finest in the land with a hope that she would one day be among them.

2

The cold air felt damp as Isra pulled her cloak around her again. She had only been here for a few hours, but already she was outside in the woods, getting acquainted with nature.

Nature was Isra's most reliable friend. She loved the way the moon shone down on the water on a cloudless night. She delighted in how the flowers bloomed just a little more beautifully as they opened up in their vibrant colors, decorating the land as spring rejoiced. She gazed fondly as orange and red leaves fell from unsuspecting trees in the height of autumn.

She looked toward one of the cherry trees as it stood alone next to the old, tall castle building. It must have been here centuries, solid as a rock but mighty in its grand finery and ornate decorations, although it could not be classed as beautiful. Ugly gargoyles blended in with much of the gray stone architecture and gaped menacingly at anyone who dared stare at them for too long. Some said the gargoyles were enchanted, but you wouldn't really know unless you got a good look at them!

She was alone in this neck of the woods in the dark of night, but she suddenly felt a presence behind her. Turning around, she was stunned to find herself staring at a fair-haired girl that looked about her age, smiling at Isra wildly, saturated in a cloak of red. She reminded Isra of a red rose that had just bloomed, opening its petals to whomever would care to witness them.

"Oh. I didn't think anyone else was out here!" the fair-haired girl uttered in response to Isra's peculiar stare.

"Neither did I," Isra responded coolly. She wasn't sure if she liked being among the company of others. She had come here to be one with the night. "Well, I guess it doesn't matter now."

The fair-haired girl pulled down her cloak to reveal more masses of golden hair going down in ringlets past her shoulders. "My name is Everilda. I'm new here," she announced with a cheery grin.

Isra smiled, although she wasn't sure why. She had never been good at connecting with those her age, always having found herself in the company of adults who were more intelligent and at her level, but she decided to be open to the possibilities that a friendship might bring.

She extended her hand warmly. "I'm Isra. I am also new. I've been a witch for many moons though!" She mused thoughtfully, having accepted that her gift was one that was not going to disappear within the fragile moments of night.

Everilda raised her eyebrow at Isra quizzically as if she didn't believe Isra. She thought, *Why would a witch be here if she's already a witch? Perhaps she's a really pretentious know-it-all that wants to advance and be higher than her peers.* Then she shrugged the thought off, moving her back closer to the cherry tree as Isra eyed her with a new sense of fascination.

"Are you connected with the ways of the craft?" Isra probed.

Everilda hesitated before answering. She had read one or two books on the subject but in her honest mindset, she hadn't done much in the way of study. Gallivanting around with young men was a far more interesting pursuit for her.

"I've read a little," Everilda stated carefully, feeling like any lack of intelligence would be deemed weak to her new friend.

Everilda changed her tone a little as she noticed the windows on the castle. They were lit up with a yellow-orange hue, like a flame. *A candle would always bring comfort in the dark,* Everilda mused to herself.

"Perhaps we should go inside?" she suggested, her blue eyes darting toward Isra trying to ascertain whether Isra was receptive or not.

Isra lowered her hood once more, revealing her long chocolate-brown hair that had intricately bundled itself together into a bun while she had her hood up.

"Perhaps that would be nice," Isra guessed, emitting a warm smile.

After all, the air was chilly and something told Isra that companionship would be nice, if only for a little while.

Everilda's chamber consisted of warm earthy colors. A beige couch was draped in orange fabric with a sweet little intricate image of a squirrel holding a nut emblazoned onto it. The kitchenette was a little room that was barely capable of holding a small stove, never mind a compact trio of wooden cupboards housing her cutlery and kitchenware.

As Isra looked on from her seated position, she spotted a red bedspread highlighting a barely lit room hosted by a small window on the left side where the entire forest in all its green natural splendor could be viewed. Isra envisioned that many cold nights could be spent watching the animals, magnificent stags and young doe mothers watching over their young prancing around the bluebells in the midst of night's cover.

Everilda didn't strike Isra as an individual that would happily step into the throes of nature, dancing in the twilight. Isra spied Everilda admiring herself in a tall, ornate mirror, preening her long blonde hair as she mouthed something to herself. Isra couldn't make out what it was, but she presumed Everilda was only talking to her reflection and doubted that she had seen her looking over from the couch in which she was sat upon.

Everilda came back into the lounge and smiled. "Shall I make some tea?" She grinned, enthusiastically.

"Sure," Isra replied.

She noted a warmth in Everilda's demeanor. Every single item down to the cute squirrel on the couch portrayed an air of warmth and earthiness. Her place was very homely indeed. It had a vibe that said that home was everything. Perhaps in Everilda's mind, the home was far greater than any happiness.

The notion was something Isra hadn't seen in a girl her age; come to think of it, Isra hadn't been acquainted with any girls her own age for many moons, but circumstances be what they must, she thought quietly to herself as Everilda busied herself getting various accompanying tea things out of the cupboard in preparation to make the tea.

Everilda laid out an elegant spread on a small coffee table by Isra's feet. The cups and saucers all painted with sweet little rosebuds and vintage serene colors looked a little out of place compared with all the red, orange, and earth tones that dominated the rest of her home. Everilda was the first to pipe up, eager for avid conversation since Isra sat quietly drinking her tea through pursed lips. Even the orange tea had a fragrant, spicy flavor that reminded Isra of the earthy vibe even more so.

"So, what brought you to our neck of the woods?" Everilda probed a little too eagerly for Isra's liking.

Isra didn't answer at first. She was a little perturbed by the remark. Surely one would come to a coven because of the purpose of learning magic. What other reason could there be for one to come? But she translated that Everilda was a gossip of sorts despite her warm, kindhearted nature, and that gossip would fuel the flames in Everilda's hearty fire.

"I came here to hone my craft, to excel in what I was born with," Isra responded coolly. She then paused for a moment before confessing rather abruptly, "Let's face it. I can't escape my fate even if I attempted to. Magic will always be in my blood. I will always be a witch."

Everilda raised a stern eyebrow but maintained her sense of

humor as she admitted, "I've barely read any books, let alone spell books."

Isra didn't really know where to look, as during most of her life she'd always read something. Whether it was reference related or something less stimulating, she'd always found the time to read. She found that someone joining a coven and not really reading anything was a little odd, but she forced herself to sit tight, resisting the urge to challenge Everilda's lack of intellect. However, it was clear as she sat on the couch that she was very bugged by it.

"Interesting," Isra concluded, not saying anything else. She felt the subject of conversation was becoming dull and so her mind was elsewhere.

Everilda changed the tone as she questioned, "So, have you met any boys yet? I hear there are many handsome young men out here!"

Isra shifted a little in her position, feeling uncomfortable at the prospect. She wasn't here to meet boys and so this was a bit off the level for her, plus she was a virgin so that was above her level of sacred ground. She wouldn't go with a boy unless she believed she was in love with him, or for reasons of similar latitude. That was her philosophy.

"I'm not really here to meet boys!" Isra finally stated a little too firmly.

Everilda looked taken aback as if some part of her had been greatly offended. She admitted, "Well, I'm always with a boy in one way or another!"

Isra resisted the urge to ask what "one way or another" might entail, simply sipping her tea instead.

"So, you're a virgin then?" Everilda inquired with a beaming smile plastered across her face, like such a thing was abhorrent or not normal for a girl of seventeen to be still pure in her body.

Everilda acted as if this was something so ingratiatingly wrong that someone who actively pursued this vocation should be scolded or worse cajoled about, but Isra said nothing, maintaining her strong hold on silence. It seemed to be her greatest strength against Everilda's lack of wit.

This social occasion with Everilda was getting more and more irritating for Isra, but she kept her mouth shut, aligning her heart with her mind because that is what would get her through in the weeks to come.

3

———————

Winds howled from outside as a hustle of bodies hurried into the dormant room where a peculiar looking owl perched on a desk as a very tall man with jet black hair and pale blue eyes entered.

Voices whispered as the man got closer to the desk, signaling something to the owl that narrowed its eyes and fluttered away from the desk in response. The man stood up in front of the huddle of black flowing skirts that had meticulously arranged themselves on the cold stone floor at once and introduced himself.

"Good morning, all you young witches! Let me introduce myself. I am Magnus Zul Wingdom. No, it's not some weird lineage; it's just my name. I am the head warlock of this coven and also its leader." He boomed in a manner that wasn't very subtle as a dozen female eyes glazed over in his direction.

He paused to take a breath before proceeding further and then articulated, "If any issues arise and they are worthy of resolve, it is me that you come to, understand?"

The room wasn't sure if that was truly a question, or if this pompous man was telling them that it was a definitive yes, but a "do not ask any questions for this is the way of it, so shut up and be done or else" kind of answer.

A sarcastic voice at the back of the room whispered less than tactfully, "Oh, he drones on and on, doesn't he? I bet he's a barrel of laughs at a witch hunt!" Another voice launched into high-pitched laughter. These voices went unnoticed until the voice at the back caused further laughter to erupt as she twiddled her shimmery blonde hair. "I know a way to zest up his dull exterior! Hey, I bet he'd make a nice measly worm!" she finished bluntly.

This remark was just the ticket for Isra who immediately sank flustering into a fit of giggles at Everilda's concoction of imagining Magnus Wingdom as a sour faced worm! She had to admit, it was a very comical sight.

Yes, Isra and her newly acquainted pal Everilda were mocking poor old Magnus who was not amused with their insulting jibes as he glared at them both with a stern stare. Not that Isra was doing much insulting of course, but she was laughing along with Everilda's cruel yet highly entertaining joke nonetheless.

Unfortunately for Isra and Everilda, Magnus had heard this commentary, fiercely walking over to the two ladies. They stopped, mid glare, only focused on him as he eyed them both suspiciously as they sat quietly, laying in wait for his wrath.

He stooped over them and spoke coherently as he addressed Isra and Everilda. "So, my young firebreds, you think it is amusing to mock leaders of your coven with sordid jokes?" he asked immediately.

Both Isra and Everilda locked eyes, doing their utmost not to break out into hilarity again. "No, sir. We would not do a thing like that. Not at all!" Isra piped up, holding a firm hand across her throat in an attempt to stifle the giggles.

Magnus turned to face Everilda, feasting his stern blue eyes on the blonde as she stared back at him in response. Her pupils dilated as she looked at him in wonder, imagining he was going to get angry as he gave her a stare that reminded her of the stare wild animals give just before they sink their teeth into their innocent prey. She felt like she was sheepishly peering up at the cruel eyes of a predator.

"No, sir. We would not contemplate a thing like that. No. Certainly not!" Everilda insisted although she didn't believe what she was saying and neither did Isra, who had yet again sank into further laughter, placing her hand upon her mouth as the giggles continued.

This outburst did nothing for the two witches except provoke Magnus Wingdom. His cheeks turned as red as a beetroot before he erupted furiously. "You two ladies will come to see me after this session has finished. Perhaps then you will understand that insulting faculty members is not appropriate behavior!"

He returned to his stage at the front of the room, addressing the rest of the coven almost as if the entire event had never commenced. But who was he kidding? The newest students in his coven had just made a mockery out of him.

Everilda and Isra giggled as they laid spread out on the grassy bank, their blonde and chocolate-brown hair lingering respectively behind them as they stared into nothing while stuck in conspicuous fits of tremendous laughter.

The amusement hadn't worn off from Everilda's unpredictable outburst of wanting to turn Magnus Wingdom in a worm. It was so comical that it had resulted in the normally reserved Isra coming out spouting with the laughs as well.

Everilda didn't actually know anything about transformation so her joke was purely an idea, nothing else. She'd never had any experience in the art of spellcraft nor did she partake in ritualistic pursuits, but magic was hereditary in her family line, descending from the side of her mother who was controversially a gypsy. There was also some interesting mix-breeding, as Everilda's father Damien was a well feared and respected warlock.

Even more intriguing, Everilda's family lines on her father's side were strongly held Christians. Especially her paternal grandmother Marie, who had hoped her son would too be a Christian, but she'd failed to take into account that like his father before him, he too would become a most powerful sorcerer. Everilda's father had left just a year after Everilda was born.

She had met her father once when she was about nine years old. He was hardly caring. He had been cold in his communication, telling her to write to him which Everilda had done because she so deeply wanted the man to love and cherish her. Alas, it was not meant to be as the letters stopped without warning and Everilda took it upon herself to never make an effort with another family member again, that way she could never be hurt or betrayed by someone she loved.

This resolve was good, until Evie's mother developed an illness a few short months later. Because Everilda was so vengeful toward her mother due to an argument they'd had, she missed most of the moments of her mother's life. It was expected that as the eldest daughter, Everilda should have been around to help her mother recuperate while she regained her strength.

Everilda didn't establish communication with her mother again until around her sixteenth birthday, but even then, relations with her family were strained. That didn't matter to Everilda.

She was making a life of her own, rebelling against her father's high hopes for her and going against her mother's spiritual principles by taking an interest in the darker side of magic. She was further constructing rebellion by enrolling at Wingdom's Academy with the idea that she would properly learn her craft.

Everilda made out that she didn't care about magic and she didn't really, but she did want to use it for her greatest good. Not anyone else's but her own. She was very selfish in that manner. And although that made her dangerous in some minds, she really didn't care for their opinions. She was going to get what she wanted and she didn't mind what it took to get there.

Isra was daydreaming, totally amiss to Everilda's wearisome thoughts as she stared into the bleak, blue sky that was slowly immersing itself into a shade of gray. Clouds behind it were merging closer with the dank sky as she felt a warm, humid air across her skin. *It's going to rain*, Isra thought quietly to herself.

She looked across at Everilda, who seemed to be blissfully unaware that the sky had taken a darker turn for the worse, so Isra scrambled around inside her pockets, reaching for something as she concentrated. Before Everilda knew what was happening, a solid blue and gray rock hit Everilda's knee with a thud.

"Owww!" She wailed at the pain that had just struck her knee. "What did you do that for? I was thinking!" Everilda exclaimed, clutching a hand to her sore knee and rubbing it tenderly.

"Apparently, you were thinking too much! You didn't even notice the sky was graying over, beckoning in the rain!" Isra giggled as Everilda looked up at the sky, confirming Isra's words.

"Oh, that's a storm cloud, all right! I'm sorry. I was a little preoccupied," Everilda explained, as she felt like she may be a watery cloud about to erupt into a terrifying storm herself.

Everilda had only known Isra for a few short days and already many facets of the witch's personality were beginning to show in her cheerful, overly exerting exterior. Isra was ahead of her in studies whereas Everilda was more focused on what handsome young stag she could hook up with after her lessons of magic and drudgery were over.

Isra didn't share Everilda's belief that men were the delectable golden apple upon the tree of life, however. Isra saw them more as forbidden fruit that hung from crooked branches, luring in their feminine victims with even greater temptations.

Isra had never kissed a man in her entire existence, never mind pursued a man. She just didn't have the interest. Everilda was her opposite in this respect as she was always off gallivanting with a man, sometimes creeping back into her chamber in the early hours just as the moon was dying.

Isra smiled as she reflected upon Everilda's distracted frame of mind. "I noticed," she uttered firmly.

The idle notion that Everilda was fixed upon her once again crossed her mind. A gaze in fascination or something more profound? Isra didn't know. Isra did know that there was something about her that roused Everilda's jealous tendencies. It was because

Isra reminded Everilda of everything she was not. Whether that was going to be a fatality as far as their friendship was concerned, nobody knew.

Isra guessed that if something was going to manifest in the manner of a confrontation between herself and her friend, she would deal with it when that time arose, but for now, it wasn't an immediate concern so she brushed those worries aside.

4

Isra's chocolate-brown hair swayed back and forth in time with the wind as she brushed wild hairs out of her eyes, pushing them to the side of her face as she sat upon a tree stump waiting. She was growing impatient as she looked ahead of herself, wondering what was keeping Everilda. The tempestuous witch had agreed to meet Isra here and she had not yet shown up.

She had been waiting in the lime green grass of the meadow for almost an hour. The sights that graced her eyes were beautifully breathtaking. The sky was a serene ocean of blue with gently tantalizing shades of turquoise that graced themselves behind the sun's rays. Poppies the color of delicious cherries dominated the green pasture, standing out amongst all the greenery.

Isra lifted herself up from the tree stump where she had been sitting all this time, preparing to leave, when something tapped her on the shoulder. The tap had startled her and she fell back onto the stump in horror, staring back at the stranger with deep intimidation.

"Oh my! I'm sorry. I didn't mean to frighten you!" the stranger responded in an apologetic manner, lifting his black bowler hat from his head to reveal a mass of short, black, curly hair. The curls stopped at his earlobes.

Isra straightened herself, looking at the stranger with avid curiosity and wondering how such a fine specimen of a man had found himself in this unattended pasture all alone. He was dressed almost completely in black with a white shirt peeking amongst the black jacket and formal trousers, all of which were shrouded by a generously large black tailcoat.

"Oh, it wasn't that!" she said slowly, brushing a stray hair aside from her face.

"Oh," the man uttered.

He had a rather strange expression on his face. His eyes were narrowed and his brow furrowed. He was not sure whether he had greatly offended this young lady, but some perseverance was inside him so he continued to feed his intrigued mind by conversing with her. "Well, if you don't mind me asking, what was it?" he inquired with a wistful look in his eye.

Isra replied to his bold stare with one of her own as she made heed to discreetly lift up the hem of her dress, allowing her to take her eyes off the man for a moment. "I thought I was alone here," Isra uttered, not knowing why he was asking her all these questions.

"Ah, and I disturbed you!" he concurred, turning his body to the right as he felt like he should speed away from the scene immediately, having bothered the beautiful young lady long enough already.

"No..." Isra answered. She moved closer to the man, allowing her hand to gently touch the side of his face before she moved it away momentarily.

This was totally unorthodox, touching a stranger whom she had only just met, but she felt something about this man. Something special. Something that was dark and mysterious, but could lure you in like an eagle seeking its unworthy prey. She felt captivated by him although she couldn't understand why. She knew she could stare into those dazzling brown eyes of his for endless hours, bewitched by his very strong features.

Isra imagined herself in a tunnel as she found her way inside his deep eyes wondering what stories they would tell. It was as though she'd found herself in a trance-like state. Peculiar as it was, she felt no magic from this man and so she presumed him to be mortal. But still, there was something intriguing visually about him.

Her mind could have wandered further but she was stopped in mid thought as a thunder clap echoed across the sky. Rain cascaded down from the heavens as she and the stranger were engulfed in the center of the storm cloud. Bemused, she turned to the stranger at once, seemingly flushed as she tried to get herself together. Her skin was dripping. Being out in the open, she had no protection from nature's ailments.

"It seems we've hit a storm cloud, we should find shelter!" Isra said at once, waiting for the dark, handsome stranger to emit something worthy of a response.

"Yes, I quite agree. I didn't expect it to rain," the stranger confessed, feeling slightly embarrassed as his clothes were soaked through. His hair fell down in a flat clump on top of his head as the rain continued to hammer down.

"I know some place where we can be sheltered, but it's a little ways from here. By the way, what is your name?" Isra pressed, looking eager to escape from the rain.

As the rain pelted down on their heads, Isra looked at the man. She felt bad treating this man like a stranger. A stranger she felt quite acquainted with despite only meeting him a few minutes ago.

"Jonathan," he uttered. He extended his hand to Isra with a friendly grin.

She looked at him for a moment, seeming a bit perturbed at him giving his hand to her, but she pushed the thought away and brought her wrist forward. Jonathan looked into Isra's eyes and smiled before taking her hand and delicately pressing his lips onto it. Isra was a little taken aback with this and wanted to pull her hand away, but he released her hand as soon as he saw her cheeks go apple red.

"I'm sorry," he mumbled.

"It's quite fine. I'm just not used to strangers taking my hand, bestowing it with their ... sweet kiss!" She stopped, feeling flushed. "I'm Isra," she finished, moving closer to him.

It was now that he got a real good look at her. She stood inches away from him. He marveled at the way the weather had drenched her skin and clothing and still she looked enchanting. Jonathan couldn't tell if she was scared or embarrassed. Her body language was incredibly hard to read. All he could see was her shy eyes, fluttering back and forth in between blinks. Most of her was hidden, like it was secluded away safely behind a strong wall, and that wall was impossible to break down.

Thinking about it, Jonathan guessed that Isra was a reserved girl with very little time for debauchery or anything that could be considered fun. He imagined that she would turn her nose up at anything that made itself seem out of the ordinary. She presented herself as a prim and proper girl to him as he glossed over her fine clothing and the way her chocolate-brown hair was combed but still hung loosely down her shoulders even when it was sticking to her skin, soaking wet from the downpour.

"Well, Isra, I must say it is an honor to meet you," Jonathan gushed, his gaze fleeting from her own as they stood getting saturated in the rain. Jonathan raised an eyebrow over Isra, placing a hand to his lips. "So, you say you know a place where we can go safely out of the torrential rains? I, for one, hate being saturated in nature's most vile of emotions," he remarked, grimacing at her.

His repulsed look made Isra laugh a little. How disgusted he looked, judging by the scowl of displeasure that was stoned upon him.

It's only a little water, dear, Isra thought to herself with a snide chuckle. *Calm yourself! What's the worst it can do? Soak you to your weary bones?*

She was glad Jonathan could not hear her thoughts for she found herself being a little too amused at her own theoretical question. At first glance, Isra thought Jonathan was a rather pompous young man, but yet there was some irresistible charm to him as he stood wet in his black formal attire, the material sticking to him. Black was not the best color to wear when the heavens were opening up and unleashing their fury.

"Yes, I do, but it's a little ways from here. Don't worry, I'll show you the way," Isra offered, extending her hand in a welcoming gesture of friendship to this handsome stranger that she had only just met.

Don't tell me he's some handsome prince from a neighboring realm! she cajoled to herself in mid thought. *It would be just my luck to fall for someone like that. And a person like that I definitely cannot have. Still, I cannot wait to tell Everilda about this!* Isra mused to herself with a sly chuckle as she carefully led Jonathan away from the meadow into drier terrain.

5

Jonathan turned to Isra in a thoughtful gaze. Being huddled up to her in the stone shelter suddenly gave him perspective on how dainty she truly was, barely even formed as a woman. Tiny, but yet those piercing green eyes of hers made up for her lack of womanly figure. Jonathan figured that although Isra was young, maybe she'd grow into a more feminine form, but he guessed he didn't need to worry about such details now since the rain was just about to stop.

Taking a peek from one of the stone pillars, Jonathan remarked with a casual tone, "The rain seems to have died down. How about I get you home?" to Isra. His face was calm and collected, not at all mocking. Oh, golly. He was serious.

Isra blushed beet red. She'd never had a man take interest in her before, never mind one who wanted to escort her home. This was an experience of a hereditary kind, like a heart attack. And like someone who was about to suffer heart failure, she worried she would suddenly clutch her chest and collapse to the ground. The shock of it was prominent in her facial expression. Isra had no inclination of what she should do in this awkward situation, but she felt it would be impolite if she refused Jonathan's kind invitation.

Here was a man she had only just met and already he was being incredibly forward with her. A nonchalant feeling surged through Isra's veins. Her heart skipped a beat. The feeling put her off guard, as she was not used to it.

She swallowed her fear allowing it to escape down her throat as she emitted, "I guess that would be acceptable." It was formal in tone as if she had just received an indecent proposal and was in two minds whether to accept it.

Jonathan, however, was more friendly, gracing her with a warm smile, something that distinctly reminded Isra of wit and happy thoughts. A person who had much pride and ambition in themselves, although that was hidden under a dark exterior of self loathing and hatred was the thought it conjured for her. He was someone that had attacked himself in a feeble attempt to back away from years of control, probably rooted from his upbringing.

"Good," Jonathan replied. He was eager as he reached for her hand, snatching it away before Isra had the chance to rebuff his advances.

I like this woman. I hope she is receptive to my devotion, he thought absentmindedly to himself while Isra led the way with her hand clutched in his, journeying with her on their way back to Wingdom's Academy.

"I really hope to be able to see you again," Jonathan whispered in Isra's direction.

Isra was perplexed, not knowing whether she should speak out and rightly decline his offer or shut up and wonder what seeing him again would be like. It appeared as if Jonathan had the intention, or want, to court her. She had never been taken astray by a man before. Oh gosh, this was so strange. What would she say? How would she behave around a man in a relationship? Just the idea of it made her squirm inside. Knowing that she was used to being alone without the need for another's company, it didn't bear thought.

The chocolate-brown strands of Isra's long hair swayed gently in the wind. The valiant building of Wingdom's Academy stood out like the eyesore it was, gray and dim with those grotesque gargoyles hanging around the castle like something really horrid that should have been vanquished long ago.

She turned to Jonathan in a thoughtful gaze. Her emerald eyes blended into his as she examined everything that resided inside them. She had to admit that she felt quite entranced by Jonathan looking at him this way. Those warm brown eyes of his felt like they were spinning as she dug deep into them.

"You'd like for us to meet again?" Isra questioned with a furrowed brow.

She was already questioning everything about Jonathan. Jonathan barely had a chance to court her. She was sending any potential romance right into oblivion with this attitude toward love and men. Analyzing Jonathan's intentions toward her and his desires for her was something she really just couldn't help.

"Yes," he answered promptly before stopping himself to pause. "Why? Is there something wrong with that?" Jonathan posed in Isra's direction as if he was asking her if she felt there was something incorrect about his wish to see her more.

"No. It's just..." Isra trailed off. She was unable to speak.

Jonathan had his eyes all over her. He was scrutinizing every part of her. What was it about this woman? This shy yet insecure demeanor that showed so much vulnerability but yet she kept herself so damn hidden, like a precious artifact that had barely seen the light of the day yet could be ever so gleaming if the right soul laid his hands all over it.

Jonathan found Isra quite fascinating. A feeble curiosity inside him was piquing now. Despite her closed off exterior, he was keen to learn what really lurked behind her cold mannerisms and the way she spoke so formally. *There must be something quite enchanting deep down in her, but only one man could be so lucky to reach it,* Jonathan thought quietly to himself, awaiting Isra's answer.

"I've never been with a man before," she confessed meekly, looking right into his warm brown eyes.

She was afraid now. Her emerald eyes darkened as the skies above her descended into dark gray clouds smothering any deep blue as quick as it could. This small act of nature symbolized her fears. Isra looked at Jonathan scared, almost as if a tidal wave would collide fiercely with the castle at any moment even though there was absolutely no likelihood of that.

Okay, why in all the heavens did I just say that? Now he will think I am some precious, prim and proper girl, shadowed away from boys and secluded by loneliness and isolation. Oh, scold me! Isra cursed herself in her thoughts.

"I see," Jonathan replied. "Well, let's see if we can change that."

Isra said nothing, simply looking at Jonathan. She then looked ahead at one of the top windows of Wingdom's Academy. The longing to get back to her own room was increasing as she felt pins and needles in her legs. The need to disappear without saying goodbye was so tempting, but she felt she had to be polite.

"Well, I must go," she said, pulling away from Jonathan at once, not giving him the chance to grab her unwillingly.

Isra's shimmering green eyes darted across to the gray stone steps at the entrance to the castle before glancing back at Jonathan. This was her escape plan. Isra was hoping Jonathan would get the hint that she had to go inside, getting away from him into a more familiar atmosphere, somewhere where she could relax and ponder the whole event.

"I understand," Jonathan uttered to her. "I presume this is a satisfactory place for us to meet again?" he pressed as he gave her some space, backing away a step. He realized his presence was a little overwhelming for her and he certainly didn't want to scare her off now before she had given him a fair trial.

"Yes. I would say it is an acceptable place to rendezvous," Isra answered before ascending up the gray steps leaving Jonathan unable to follow.

All Jonathan could do was watch as she vanished through what appeared to be a very narrow wooden door into a universe he could only dream of since males that weren't teachers were strictly forbidden from entering Wingdom's Academy.

EVERILDA SAT BACK against her red couch, relaxed and in the state that she might drift off to a slumber when suddenly a loud bang jolted her out of any sleeping plans. The door to Everilda's chamber swung upon violently, slamming across the stone wall as someone happily made their way inside.

Isra came crashing through like an excited child, jumping about, hardly able to contain it in her. She beamed with joy. Everilda only had to merely glance at Isra to know why her friend was suddenly on cloud nine.

Oh, and I thought she didn't like boys! Everilda mocked Isra silently in her thoughts. *No matter, let's hear the dreary or perhaps wonderful tale!*

Isra didn't even sit down, much to the grimace in Everilda who would have done anything to get Isra to stay still even if it was only for a moment. Isra's happy, bouncy state made Everilda feel dizzy. Finally, Everilda had enough of it, pointing at the settee for Isra to sit down upon.

"Please, calm yourself and take a seat. You are making the room spin!" Everilda said with a slight twang in her tone. A hint of bitterness could be detected as if she resented Isra being happy.

"Sorry," Isra muttered, planting herself on the red couch next to Everilda.

There was a plausible silence in the air between the two young women. Everilda glanced across at Isra with an amused expression. It was as though Everilda didn't think Isra could indeed be happy or smile. Everilda didn't think she was inaccurate in saying that this was the first time she had witnessed Isra in this state of being. And it was bewildering and yet enchanting at the same time. There was something novel in the way Isra couldn't sit still. The excitable, childlike energy came off her like she was in another realm with dreamlike imagery of unicorns, rainbows, and sweet, fluffy pink clouds.

"Out with it!" Everilda chortled with snide laughter, smiling at

Isra. "Come on Isra, I have never seen you like this. Please do tell me everything," she urged.

"All right," Isra agreed. She seemed less flustered now and somewhat complacent and in control of her behavior. "You left me out in the rain awaiting your presence..." Isra trailed off, remembering how annoyed she was that Everilda had left her out in the lurch like that. "But this handsome stranger turned up out of nowhere. I found him to be quite formal. He was begrudged that his fancy suit was getting all soggy in the earth's dismal torrent..."

Once again Isra had gone off track, her mind elsewhere as she recalled the experience of meeting Jonathan, every facet of the encounter running through her mind. As strange as it was, there was also something attractive about Jonathan. Okay, so he was pompous and self gratifying, anxious that a few measly raindrops had splattered his perfect dressy suit, but other than that there was a handsome yet mesmerizing charm about him, almost as if he just flicked a switch and suddenly it would come into being. He was all rugged and rough around the edges with a crude smile that would make women crawl to him on their hands and knees. Not that Isra would crawl to him at his wish, you understand, but she did see the charm in Jonathan.

"Yes? And then what commenced?" Everilda coaxed. The irritation was beginning to blow up as Isra stalled more and more. *It must be so fancy for one to just drift off in their little bubble whenever they please, but you should remember something called reality,* Everilda remarked with hostility toward Isra in her thoughts.

There were quite a few distinct traits in Isra that Everilda found absolutely unfathomable. Some would even say that Everilda hated some of the more mushy aspects of Isra's personality, the pieces of Isra that made her what she was: sweet, kind, good. Isra was an innocent that had yet to taste any real sense of living; well, in Everilda's opinion, anyway.

Isra realized she had gone off track into a deep fountain of imagination again, blushing as she looked dewy-eyed up at Everilda. *Oh no, there's that look. Now where have I seen that before? Oh gosh. I know. That's the insatiable glance one gives when love is present in their veins,* Everilda mocked quietly to herself.

"Sorry," Isra explained herself to Everilda. "He ... Well, Jonathan because that is his name, startled me. I wasn't expecting to find anyone else there, so he unnerved me a little," Isra stated, recalling how it happened when Jonathan suddenly came at her.

"But then we were talking, and I don't know. There was just something really intriguing about him. He escorted me back here this evening. He has expressed his need to see me again, but honestly Evie, I ran in before he had the chance to kiss my hand."

She seemed flustered as she spoke. It was likely the nerves of not knowing what would happen if she had allowed Jonathan to kiss her. Everilda raised a stern eyebrow at Isra. Finally, the conversation was peaking and they were getting somewhere. That was the trouble with Isra, she'd always go off on a tangent and they'd get halfway, seeming like it took forever to get to the truly significant and important parts.

"I would presume you are intrigued because you have a fondness for this man, Isra. A caring. Some deep-seated feeling. Something you have never experienced, and so to you it can appear foreign," Everilda told Isra.

Isra said nothing, just sat on Everilda's settee in blissful silence, clearly going off into her bubble that resided deep inside her imagination, a place where she was safe and secure and nobody could enter unless she permitted them, thus breaking the spell.

6

Everilda stood by the door, preening over her glossy golden curls while facing the gilded old ornate mirror. *I'm good to go,* she thought to herself with a sly grin. *There is just the matter of sneaking off into the night. Of course, Isra should be asleep at this unsightly hour.*

At least that's what Everilda was hoping for, anyway. Naturally, Everilda had deliberately left this dalliance for the small hours when there was very little chance of anyone seeing her. More importantly, Everilda didn't want her friend Isra to discover what she was up to as that would cause quite a ruckus if Isra were to catch her in the act. Everilda couldn't allow that. Neither did she want the confrontation that would come from it, and Everilda knew Isra would be extremely angry if she ever found out. Everilda was assured of that.

A loud chime bellowed from the neighboring chapel signaling that time was drawing on. Everilda would have to make a move in a moment if she was to get away unnoticed by any unsuspecting residents of Wingdom's Academy. She smiled a cheeky smile. Her sky-blue eyes glanced toward the antique clock sitting on the warm tangerine wall behind her. The sounds of the bells chiming in the distance echoed all throughout the land announcing that midnight was here at last.

She'd waited all night for this and now she was going to have her merry way without a soul knowing hither nor hair of it.

EVERILDA STOOD out in the cool evening breeze awaiting something or someone to arrive; only she didn't look like an excited child about to tear open a gift of promise and fulfillment. She lurked in the area between the trees and the unkempt wilderness, making sure she stayed out of the bright light that descended from the glittering stars above her. Although she did think they looked fanciful, Everilda certainly didn't want anything shining down on her so her face could be seen in the darkened terrain. She was decorated in a soft black dress that clung to her robust yet slim figure in all the right places. It was the perfect ensemble for one who wanted to hide under the night's coating.

Softly, footsteps could be heard behind her, gently treading across the overgrown grassy carpet surrounding the forest path. The sounds dimmed a little, and then peaked again as they grew closer before finally Everilda found herself staring at a tall man looking ravishing with untidy black hair that he'd clearly forgotten to comb.

"Jonathan." She gasped, shocked that he had actually joined her after she had summoned him so rudely.

Jonathan stepped forward, reaching for Everilda's hand. "Everi," he pronounced, blessing her hand with a graceful kiss.

Everi was the fond nickname Jonathan had given Everilda, but only he would call her it, giving even more meaning to it as if it was some secret between them although they were hardly star-crossed lovers.

Everilda was quite pleased with herself. Jonathan bent down before her, worshiping the area beneath her feet. It was quite a thrill having a man bow down to her at this level. It gave her an overwhelming sense of power, although after a few moments she found him irritating and so she waved her finger at him, making him get back up quicker than a stallion who had been scolded.

"That's better," Everilda mouthed. "Well Jonathan, you could have at least tidied your hair. What's the matter, did you think I'd be offended at you looking half presentable to the world?" She mocked him with sarcastic wit almost as though venom was poking out through her words.

"I didn't have time." Jonathan excused himself, pushing his fingers through his hair in a dire attempt to push it back in a slicked-back fashion, although judging by how hurriedly he did it he wasn't convinced it made a difference, much like anyone was trying to make themselves look half decent when they had been dragged out into the small hours to have a rather intrusive chat where nobody else could lay eyes on them.

"Why did you drag me out here, Everilda?" Jonathan questioned.

The dark umber in his eyes radiated out against the moonlight. An air of curiosity surged through him like some part of him was reaching deep into Everilda, reading every inch of her soul. Everilda straightened her glance, her eyes glossing over Jonathan's perplexed manner. It soon became clear to her that Jonathan had no idea why she had dragged him out here.

Oh dear, he's not exactly on form, she cackled to herself in her thoughts.

"I thought I'd fill you in on our little situation," Everilda muttered through pursed lips. Her expression was coarse. She wasn't smiling. "It's just, you seem to have made quite an impression on my young friend. Now, what is her name?" Everilda recited in a patronizing tone.

She was clearly expecting Jonathan to take the bait, to catch the hint while it was fresh, dangling it by his throat while he was still young enough to make the connection. But he had no idea what she was muttering about. The confused glances Jonathan threw in Everilda's direction said it all. He really wished she would get to the point instead of yammering on about matters that he had no comprehension of.

Everilda would always dawdle, diverting the course around the horse and carriage before she got to the palace. He grumbled quietly under his breath, taking heed to make sure he was not heard in either voice or thought because as amateur as Everilda was, she could smell a thought from miles away.

"Oh yes, that's it. *Isra*," Everilda finished.

Jonathan gulped. He looked as pale as a soft, fluffy white cloud. Oops. That pretty girl with the chocolate silk hair he'd met the other day was Everi's friend?

Shit. I'm in for it now. Why didn't I think? I should have realized they both went to Wingdom's Academy. But maybe I can chortle my way out of this, he thought feebly.

"Isra. That's a rather unique name. Yes, I did meet her," Jonathan announced formally. "I had no idea she was an acquaintance of yours." He stiffened, feeling a sensation in his nether regions. Just how painful it would be if Everilda chose to chastise him right here and now in the midst of the forest?

"I said she is a friend," Everilda corrected. "But it is no matter. You will let her down gently and we will not be discussing this again," she stated in a demanding manner as if she had expected him to take her word as gospel, thus compelling him to do as she demanded.

"Ah. That could be difficult," Jonathan objected while tossing Everilda a disgruntled look, taking heed that he was a few steps away from her because just about anything could set her off at this point.

In the spirit of things, Jonathan stared Everilda right in the face, further defying her because he had already done it once; now he was going to justify his choice. And what better way than to make Everilda feel small.

"I rather like Isra. She seems sweet, innocent. Everything that you and I are not. Why would I not want to carry on with what we have?"

Everilda gave Jonathan an icy stare, flashing her cold sapphire-blue eyes in deep hatred and resentment over his refusal to go along with what she wanted. Any moment now, it looked like she might blow out all her fury, thrusting it upon him.

Everilda raged deep inside her thoughts, silently fuming to

herself, for now was not the time to give mortal Jonathan the satisfaction of knowing he had gotten one over on her, royally pissing her off. No, she wasn't going to let him see that. She'd stay quiet, venting in the darkest parts of her mind while deciding how best to deal with Jonathan for his rude and most despicable behavior.

How dare he say no to ditching Isra! Oh, how dare he even suggest that we all carry on this shenanigan while Isra doesn't know the history Jonathan and I have. But I know it well enough, don't I? I was fortunate or maybe just cursed to meet this man in what can only be described as bizarre circumstances when I was lucky enough to engage his brother in that charming town, Bitterquel, a most exquisite realm where the ruggedly handsome Prince Valien gets to lord over all and sundry while doing as he pleases, exceptionally ignoring the tribulations of royal regulation.

He's a rebellious sort, but I did rather like him. Being the brother of Jonathan, I found out all too quickly how deeply besotted Jonathan was with me, much to my and Valien's dismay, but no matter. These things happen when you mix with those just as screwed up as you are. If only Valien and I had become better acquainted. Perhaps I could have tossed Jonathan away, discarding him, but I hear dear old Valien is engaged to be married now. I can safely presume that little jolly escapade is right off the menu. Shame, as he is so scrumptious.

Everilda mused about how fine Valien had looked with his sleek black hair that curled ever so slightly upon his fringe so that it gave the illusion of curls, and then how it was so soft and shiny. She imagined her fingers wading through it as she got down to the back where it was so ever elegantly shaved to perfection. It would have been marvelous if she'd ever had a chance to get a grip on the man's fine mane.

She turned back to Jonathan, quickly realizing that she had daydreamed of Valien so much she had almost forgotten about her little standoff with Jonathan.

"Oh. I'm sorry. I am a little tuckered out. It must be all this gallivanting off into the night to scold you," Everilda countered, excusing herself and hoping that she wasn't blushing a bright beet red at having fantasies of getting her hands on Valien right when Jonathan was only a few feet away from her.

Jonathan laughed, "Scold me? Oh Everi, you haven't even come close to doing that. You've barely even scratched the surface."

He chided her with flitting amusement as his dark brown umber eyes met her cold, blue spheres in a most perilous, frozen stare. If he didn't know any better he would have guessed he was looking at the gaze of a queen from a desolate, weary land, one that had once reigned and was now left to wither and die.

He paused for a moment, flinching a little as he faced her once more. "I suppose you had this all worked out. Bringing me out here where you could get me by my lonesome. And then you probably thought that you could have me held to do as you will, only you hadn't factored in that I might not agree to your demanding request. I've said it once and I could say it a hundred times. A harsh and cold heart will always succeed in building yet more ice around it."

Everilda glared at Jonathan for his remark, giving him another cold, harsh stare that could probably send him into the fiery pits of hell if she had the power to accomplish that. For now, her anger would have to suffice.

"Yes, well some creatures don't easily bow down to what is best for them," she cajoled with a stern look, twitching while she looked down, picking up the hem of her jet black dress as it trailed on the ground before her.

"Hmmm. Touché," Jonathan quipped, taking the initiative that now it was time to walk away. He'd said all he had wanted to here; there was nothing more. Absolutely no purpose in him standing in the cold terrain with a venomous creature like Everilda. No, he'd turn right around and go home.

But where was home for Jonathan? Since he had a rich brother drenched in luxury and responsibility, you'd have figured he'd have a fantastical palace somewhere with lush gardens, right? Wrong! Jonathan occupied a quaint cottage just outside of a place called Spirisity, known for mysticism and wonder. Only those truly attuned to the magics in their natural untainted form would care to know what was found there.

Jonathan's home was almost next door to the prestigious Wingdom's Academy located in the tranquil land of Seclera. It was a vast forest land, home to many that was surrounded by a wide open ocean of the same name. If you wanted to get to Wingdom's from the calm waters of Seclera, it was only a brisk five-minute walk and you were right there. Meanwhile, Jonathan's home was located just between Spirisity and Seclera, half a mile away from Seclera so he was smack bang in the middle of wall-to-wall magic whichever way he chose to go! How poetically ironic for a mortal that had no interest in magic whatsoever.

But it wasn't like he had a choice in the matter. Jonathan had lost all chances of gaining a place on the throne because their father Marco had thought Jonathan wasn't responsible enough to uphold the title. Marco felt Jonathan would bring shame upon the family name, as he was always off with some charming belle or another and getting merry in the local tavern making a fool of himself like the drunken idiot he was. So that paid to that, and Jonathan was struck off from ever laying claim to the royal throne. Sure, that pissed him off a bit, but there wasn't a single thing he could do to change Marco's decision and no point dwelling on the matter.

And there was no purpose in him standing here in this flight of fancy with Everilda, so turning his head and heading on his heels, he didn't even look at Everilda, choosing to say nothing as he walked off.

"Yes, you walk away Jonathan, but mark my words, you have not heard the last of this!" Everilda shouted after him menacingly as she watched him disappear through the mass of tall trees.

Empty threats, Everi. Cold and lifeless empty threats. Jonathan chuckled quietly as he resisted the urge to turn around and see the look on Everilda's face.

7

In the realm of Spirisity with dawn just about to break, a man looked at his antique brown wall clock with anticipation. His guest would be arriving at any moment.

What's taking him so long? Doesn't he know there are important matters to discuss? I sometimes wonder why I kept this raven under my wing when he can't even turn up on time to an arranged meeting. Carelessness, the man muttered to himself in his thoughts.

He anxiously ran his fingers through his slicked back, black hair that was perfectly kept just above his neck at the back, busily awaiting that royal blue curtain to burst open at any second when the raven would come flying in. As the man, Samuel, adjusted his silver moon-framed glasses, he shifted a little in his comfortable red velvet chair. The plush velvet cushioning supported his back as he sat slightly stiff, awaiting the news that he presumed would be welcoming. But news like this didn't come every day; maybe it wouldn't be so good after all. Only time would tell. And as for time, Astrid the raven was already late in making his appearance.

I know Astrid is probably helping himself to a lovely sample of juicy worms. That is likely why the boy is late, Samuel marveled to himself quietly in thought.

When he thought more clearly about how demanding Astrid's job was, it was easy to understand that Astrid couldn't just thrive on fresh air alone. Any raven that was Samuel's right-hand man (so to speak) would most definitely need to stop and replenish his energy, especially when you considered the importance of the roles Samuel and Astrid played in the scheme of things.

Samuel was one of the very few light bringers still operating in a densely populated area coated in magic. It was Samuel's task to reign in those who succumbed to darkness to prevent greater repercussions. No, he wasn't an angel or anything like that, but he did have an immortality about him since he had long discarded his human life long ago. Very few were aware of that detail. But the folk that were on high, metaphysically speaking, were determined to keep it that way.

The location of Samuel's headquarters was a very sparse area so unless you knew where it was, it was unlikely you'd find it unless you had razor sharp vision. For being in such an unknown place, it was a fairly decent sized gray castle that stood out like a sore thumb amongst a mass of yellow ochre flowers and emerald green grass in the not so widely known land of Spirisity. How peculiar that it was adjacent to the neighboring realm of Seclera where a certain coven could be found.

Samuel sat in his chair, twiddling his fingers and thumbs when suddenly the royal blue curtain burst open as a black raven made his long-awaited entrance.

Finally, Samuel thought to himself. *I did wonder what had happened as to why he was taking so long.*

"Astrid. It's about time you graced me with your presence," Samuel started eagerly. "Come, sit down. Take the weight off your claws."

Astrid said nothing, making haste in flying over to his master and sitting beside him on the window ledge.

"It's been an eventful night," Samuel began. "Those on high have concerns over a young witch that is headed for pure, unadulterated darkness."

"I see," Astrid answered, although there was a small pause. The raven was confused over why they had been assigned such a matter, as it was rather unorthodox to be dealing with those who were still at this time in the light. "Why is this in our domain? We only assist those that have turned and are dangerous to the realm as we know it," Astrid probed.

In the sheer knowledge of how the light versus the dark worked and had done for centuries now, they never got involved until someone had completely moved over to evil. In the universal law, the light didn't intervene until someone had completely turned their back on the light, taking advantage of the other more attractive and appealing side. The one where glossy shiny apples glittering with all their pungent ruby red tones beckoned a soul to come in and bite them. Sinking their teeth into the tasty, sweet flesh, giving in to all that temptation. All the blood lust and power that could be discovered in one fatal, delicious moment.

"It is a special case!" Samuel interjected, looking like he was about to go off on a tangent as he eyed Astrid carefully, almost the same way a father would stare at a naughty child before he delivered a harsh reprimand.

"How long have you been working for me?" Samuel questioned. "You know how it works. You understand how every facet of earth integrates with that of the metaphysical and unsavory beings that inhabit this land, and still you question the whys, wherefores, and hows. We are not in the business of how or why. We are instructed on behalf of those that are not seen or heard. The ones who fly unnoticed control our lands. We do as we are bid, for we are part of a great service that not only honors souls but saves them inadvertently from themselves ... most of the time."

"I understand," Astrid relented. "So may I ask why this witch is, as you say, 'a special case'?"

He was curious as to why something like this had been sent their way when normal procedure was to only intervene when a soul had turned to the dark, leaving absolutely no room for a reprieve whatsoever. Samuel smiled at Astrid with a coy wink and then pressed his palms together for a moment as if he was in prayer, silently mulling over Astrid's query.

"Let's just say that those on high have raised their concerns with this special lady as she is part of a prophecy that has not yet commenced," Samuel explained, noticing how Astrid looked at him in a perplexed manner.

Oh, prophecies involving a lady that has not yet turned over to the darkness. Wow she must be a major player, Astrid muttered sarcastically to himself in mid thought. *I wonder what is so mystifying about her that Samuel is keeping so tight-lipped about nearly every single facet there is to know about her. Or more precisely, not know, as he isn't letting on to anything. Is she such a firecracker that the on high are on strict orders to keep us in the dark, excuse the pun, concerning her?*

"I see. Are you going to elaborate more than that?" Astrid questioned Samuel with a curious glance.

"I will tell you her name, Astrid, but other than that I am not at liberty to reveal it at this time."

Well, okay, having a name is something I guess, Astrid thought sarcastically to himself, taking care that Samuel wasn't reading his thoughts because if Samuel got wind of Astrid's attitude, he'd be in for quite the reprimand.

Samuel looked over at Astrid giving him a burning stare as if he had deciphered what the cheeky raven had been thinking. He paused before voicing in a bold, deep voice: "Isra."

That's a sweet name for a girl about to unleash hell on earth according to those winged warriors in the know, Astrid thought. *But maybe it's a little too sweet. I guess time will only tell on what will occur with this feisty femme-fatale about to rock someone's world as she plunges headfirst into her own darkness.*

Isra hid herself under her chocolate-brown hair. The lush, glossy mass of it fell across her face as it nestled in between the hood of her jet-black cloak barely revealing her face to the world.

Since Isra was meeting Jonathan out beside the ocean that guarded the remote area of Seclera, that was hardly a problem for her. Her unruly hair could do with a tidying up, but being hidden beneath it proved to be a most useful accessory indeed since she didn't want any attention drawn to her or Jonathan.

It had barely struck dusk with the sun's leftover light just glinting onto the reflection of the water as it dissipated from the sky. If you looked up ahead, you could see splinters of reddish-orange where the daylight was finally fading, allowing the moon to rise up and bloom in her rightful spot where she would beam all night.

Isra felt anxious before leaving Wingdom's Academy. She hadn't told anyone about this liaison, not even Everilda, and she was certain it wouldn't go down well with others if she had divulged the details to anyone. Matter of fact, men were forbidden at Wingdom's, as was courting them. Isra was putting her entire magical education on the line with the chance of her being expelled from the academy if anyone ever found out about her and Jonathan. But Isra was a flighty girl full of rebellion, so she didn't mind taking the risk.

There was nothing more boring for Isra than the mundane, that dreary way of living where you did the same thing day in, day out. If she could heighten things up a notch believe me, she would every single time. Frightfully dull was never something Isra would entertain in her life. And if she ever did, you could guarantee she didn't have it for very long.

I wonder where that plucky man is, Isra thought quietly to herself, unsure when, or if, Jonathan would indeed show up. Their rendezvous had been very last minute, so she was sure if he'd decided to pursue something or someone else that she'd be the last one to know. Just as the speck of doubt entered her mind, a figure emerged from a mass of trees that guarded Seclera and the land surrounding it, Spirisity.

The two lands were joined together at the border in a sense, but at the halfway point so one land cleverly stood on the outskirts of the other. In this case, it was Spirisity, the land where the light bringers reigned and did their good work unseen and unheard by those whose souls weren't so bright. The tainted folk were not aware of Spirisity's true nature because if it was ever shaded upon what the light bringers' role was, there would be a whole lot of witches, warlocks, and the like casting out their venomous curses like begrudging moles that had never touched fire.

But anyway, Jonathan was now approaching Isra. Isra's eyes were all over him, glossing over his soft facial features as he focused and turned away from the spectacular views of the ocean that surrounded Seclera and onto Jonathan.

If you ever wanted to get away on a dark night and be somewhere alone to think, this would be the perfect location to find yourself in.

Jonathan glanced across at Isra with a warm smile, his right arm extended and ready to give her his hand when he finally got to her. It was as though he had been awaiting this moment tenderly. The charm radiated off his face, spouting out of him like vomit although most women didn't find it off-putting. Jonathan was quite the handsome and desirable sort of fellow, a man that could walk right up to a lady and something about him would just enchant her. One could wonder if he actually possessed magical powers since women found his mannerisms as well as how he spoke so formally to them entrancing.

The question that had yet to be answered was of course, had he enchanted Isra?

She was young, only having come of age at seventeen. Isra felt that yes, he was attractive, but she was still quite intimidated by Jonathan in the sense that she didn't know enough about him. It bewildered her that he was interested in making acquaintances with her, although whether she had fallen for his beguiling ways remained to be seen. Isra had agreed to meet Jonathan again so that was a small indication of mutual wanting, however he'd best keep himself and his ego grounded because she had not revealed one tiny scrap of emotion for him ... yet.

The idea that Jonathan may or may not want Isra was cast aside as she found herself thrown out of her perplexing bubble of ongoing thoughts when she realized he was bent down at her feet with his left hand placing a kiss on hers.

Oh, my goodness, he really goes all the way, Isra thought with a smile, fighting her intense urge to push his hand away as she felt herself turn bright red with embarrassment.

"Jonathan." She greeted him with a low bow. "How nice of you to grace me with your ravishing presence once more." Isra spoke to him in a tone that wouldn't have gone amiss in a stately palace. How funny when you consider she had never laid eyes on one.

"Isra, my lady. The pleasure is all mine," Jonathan insisted, standing up so he was towering over her. At six foot tall, he was of average height for a man of his age, however as he was only eighteen and he still had some growing to do, thus meaning he'd be even taller one day.

Jonathan moved away from her slightly form, standing next to her so he was parallel with her line of vision. He did this as Isra looked at him with a slightly cursed half smile like something about him irritated her. Contempt resounded in her eyes, that angry look that one would give someone when they had done something that they didn't agree with. Jonathan was not used to a woman not being unappreciative of his efforts so he said nothing, accepting his fate in the open space with her.

"It is dark," Isra observed, looking across the gleaming cobalt-blue ocean. She hadn't even realized that in the several minutes she and Jonathan had been conversing, night had overtaken them.

"Yes, it is," he agreed.

Jonathan looked at Isra with a flirtatious glance, smiling just enough to catch her attention although she was besotted with the crashing waves that stood out ahead of them. Why she would be fascinated with the ocean when he was standing beside her he could not figure out, but clearly Isra was a young woman of many unique interests.

"I was wondering if it would be too presumptuous to invite you back to my cottage? It's only a stone's throw away, but there is a warm log fire and we could have tea," he proposed with an eager enthusiasm in the hope she'd accept his basic but well-thought out offer.

Isra took her time in answering him. She carefully mulled over his proposition although unbeknownst to him, Isra was actually selectively pulling it part, analyzing his intentions. Her emerald green eyes shimmered and flitted back at him, scanning him for any signs that she shouldn't go through with this. Disappointing as it was to admit, Isra could not find any, but maybe this was her weakness for him.

Still, she was a flighty young thing bursting with enthusiasm and energy for anything that happened to come her way. And as haphazard as Jonathan had landed in her domain, Isra had to admit something about him intrigued and captivated her, although what that was she was not truly certain.

"I would presume tea with you to be satisfactory," Isra mumbled, quietly looking behind her all of a sudden as she heard a screeching sound.

"Delightful. It is settled. You will come to my humble abode," Jonathan replied in an excited tone as if some part of him had expected Isra to reject his tantalizingly irresistible offer.

What girl in her right mind would dispel the chance to have tea with a fumbling, handsome man full of himself, stuffed to the brim with a faultless ego and handsome to boot? Sure, Jonathan had his good points, such as that warm, caring personality of his that cropped up when he didn't feel the need to hide behind an overbearing inflamed personality, but it was a rare event that this man showed emotions.

"Your presence would not be welcomed at Wingdom's. It is strictly forbidden for men to be there, outside of the coven members that teach us the ways of the magics," Isra stated.

She stood calmly looking across the cold, callous seas. The waves were rough and harsh as they brushed against the remnants of whatever fine land had once been there before the ocean had catapulted it into the torrential current it was now. Isra paused, grinning as she eyed Jonathan's fleeting glance of her, feeling mischievous as she realized the full extent of the trouble they'd both be in if anyone was to catch sight of their illicit liaison.

"By me conversing with you here now, I am actually risking

banishment from the establishment by Magnus Wingdom himself," Isra added dryly, catching sight of the area around her and fearing that she might be caught at any moment by some unsuspecting onlooker. She had already heard something in the distance so it wasn't paranoia for her to think that someone was watching her.

However unbeknownst to her, someone was.

8

The raven dusted off his feathers before preparing to take flight again. He had to be careful because he had been undertaking a very important mission, keeping a vigil on the activities of a new player that was rumored to come into darkness.

Astrid, as he was named, had been ordered to keep watch on the person his master believed would soon be unleashing hell unto the world, a witch that went by the name of Isra. It was a sweet name that meant lady of the night which was very appropriate when you considered that she was going to be someone that would soon strike a bargain with darkness, becoming one with it.

Astrid had been watching Isra with much avid fascination, curious as to how this sweet yet regal creature was going to succumb to the dark side. But Astrid knew better than to criticize the prophecies that came from those in the know, the light bringers to be precise. Astrid himself knew the cost of ignoring that which is in front of your own eyes, so it wasn't a mistake he was going to make again in a hurry.

Astrid had been watching Isra and the male companion of hers for about an hour now, flying overhead subtly enough so he could keep her in his sights but not be seen by anyone. He had just been taking a pit stop to rest his tired feathers when he suddenly saw Isra and the male, some tall man with lavish short black hair the color of coals stride down the path carelessly, not aware that someone's beady golden eyes were all over them at this very moment.

Acting quickly, Astrid arched his back, stretching out his wings as he launched into the murky midnight-blue translucent cover of night.

Luckily for Astrid and his little stalking mission, there were a lot of fluffy opalescent clouds tonight so he could flutter in between them and not be visible. This was the ideal weather for Astrid to keep tabs on Isra when he had almost lost sight of her already. Astrid had quickly found out that the young witch in training was fast paced and didn't dawdle when she walked.

It was bewildering to Astrid as to how he was going to keep up his spying mission with his target being so full of abundant energy. But orders were orders, so Astrid would have to up his game with Isra which was challenging as he only had his wings to do that, whereas this not yet immortal creature had two fine, slim legs of which she could get away from his wary eyes very quickly.

There she was, such a fragile yet strong looking form of a girl. That chocolate-brown hair of hers uncurled at the unruly ends so effortlessly, like silk. Then there were those sharp emerald green eyes that could light up a grim pathway if you went wandering down one.

I don't understand what I am meant to do in relation to her, but so far I see nothing dark. She's just a sweet girl. Full of innocence. Just what could taint a soul like this I do not know, Astrid commented in his thoughts, clearly feeling abrasive toward the idea that the on high felt that Isra could be headed for darkness.

Astrid considered the situation as he watched Isra and the man she was with, Jonathan, stop just by a quaint cottage. Golly, they'd only been strolling along a moment ago and now they were entering this sweet little cottage.

It wasn't much really when you looked at it. It didn't have any kind of irresistible charm like the type of cottage where roses were strewn upon the door, climbing across the walls because they were growing wildly without assistance. No, Jonathan's cottage had pale peach walls on the outside with ivory window frames and the antique door was just a plain old brown oak with a gold tapper. Nothing special at all.

You'd have thought he'd have something that made the place seem homely but no, even the garden was lacking in potential with just a small patch of soil that seemed to have what looked like murky green weeds popping out their heads above it in a frenzy.

Astrid watched as Jonathan and Isra made their way through the brown oak door with it shutting behind them. Okay, so now Astrid had to seize his position, taking refuge on the iron window frame, sitting at the edge so that he was not seen. For this was a reconnaissance mission to gain intelligence on the witch, and he had to be careful not to blow his cover.

Leaning in through a tiny crack of which the window was ajar, Astrid's beady golden eye surveyed over the open-spaced living area where Jonathan was now bringing two steaming mugs of what appeared to be some hot beverage judging by the gray steam coming from the cups. Astrid wasn't close enough to see exactly what it was, but from the aroma it was giving off it seemed to be fragrant and woody. Perhaps a faint whiff of cinnamon, although it was hard to tell.

Anyway, what Isra and Jonathan were drinking wasn't important. The point of this little mission was to gather information on Isra and her life before her supposed reign in dark peril. It was crucial that Astrid didn't get sidetracked with things that weren't relevant to his cause.

Jonathan sat down next to Isra on a musty, old, cream couch. Again, he didn't have much to shout about when it came to material things and this old piece of furniture screamed it from the bellows. It was saturated with what looked like ochre yellow and rich brown stains and had rips in the upholstery. Even the fabric on the legs of the couch was fraying at the ends. It looked rather pathetic really.

Isra, on the other hand, was being docile, not uttering a word. She simply sat in solemn silence with this man that she believed wanted to court her. But because she was a shy shadow of a girl; she remained mute, not really knowing what she should say.

Naturally Jonathan had to engineer the conversation because Isra wasn't going to. "So how is the tea?" he inquired with a friendly glance over at Isra who was sipping her spiced apple tea through pursed lips.

Jonathan seemed a little nervous, maybe even wary of Isra in some respect. The chestnut color in his eyes darkened a little as his pupils widened. The interpretation that Astrid could make out was that Jonathan was on edge over what Isra may not do. More so, Astrid found that amusing since Jonathan had led Isra here on a merry dance away from the seclusion of the mundane gray halls back at Wingdom's Academy.

"It's fine," Isra replied, placing her cup down on the table.

Isra, who was in need of a fine distraction, glanced toward the pale walls surrounding her. Dingy beige with barely-there elements of brown covered the interior of Jonathan's cottage. Some would say it had character, and others would mock him for not having a pot to piss in.

"It's a little bare in here, isn't it?" Isra observed. She regarded Jonathan in a perplexed manner as if she had expected something more from his home.

Jonathan gave Isra a smug look like he owned the world all of a sudden, thinking he was lording over any feminine presence that should be lucky enough to come near him. "What I lack in splendor is replaced by my enthralling and witty personality," Jonathan retorted with a confident grin broadening his cheeks.

"Hmm," Isra sounded out as if she wasn't completely convinced. Clearly Jonathan's elongating charms weren't making much of an impression on her. "I expected more for someone like yourself," Isra explained as she lifted herself up from the grotesque couch.

She moved over to the plain walls, placing her palm across them as if she was feeling out for something in particular. Isra closed her eyes, only just for a moment, like she was sensing something or some kind of energy. Isra was a witch after all, so communing with the spirits was expected, right?

However, Jonathan found this behavior of hers rather odd. She stood silently with her hand on the wall before she involuntarily removed her hand and sat back down next to him on the couch.

This girl sure is strange, Jonathan muttered to himself discreetly in his thoughts. *I guess I have to be careful with her. If she has a way to communicate with things that cannot be seen by the naked eye, I could be in a hell of a lot of trouble if I step outside the lines of what she deems to be right.*

Astrid agreed with Jonathan in his own thought train. *Yes, in a lot of trouble you may find yourself indeed! She does strike me as a mighty creature. Darkness or no darkness. My goodness, if you piss her off, I shall be there to see it. It's a show worth watching especially for someone as despicable as you,* Astrid added with a condescending tone.

The raven was still spying on Isra. Astrid cleverly sat on the edge of the window while listening in to Jonathan and Isra as they sat barely speaking in his living area, but Astrid could read Jonathan's thoughts with little effort. A gracious gift some might say, but ravens were known for being fine messengers, able to converse through any kind of supernatural means. Astrid had a tremendous talent for reading any soul he came into contact with. He could dissect every little thought that popped into a person's or animal's mind, but humans were his most fun ones to analyze.

Astrid found the ways and acts of the humans highly entertaining. It transfixed him how so many humanized minds were fascinating domes of unearthed secrets. Baffling as they were for people, they sure were intriguing.

It's enchanting, I must say. Here you invited the girl to your home, and she hardly utters a word to you. Are you that tedious, dear mortal? Astrid chuckled as he suddenly caught sight of Isra's primitive gaze. Her sharp green eyes sparkling like emeralds almost met him for a second, but the raven was quick to duck out of her line of vision.

"Golly, that was a close one!" Astrid muttered. "I must be stealthier with this lady because she has eyesight that is incredibly heightened, and…" Astrid trailed off, pausing. He realized if he was to continue to survey Isra, he needed to make haste to ensure he was not caught under any circumstance. "If she were to catch me, well, Samuel would not be best pleased."

Astrid paused again. It dawned on him that Samuel would be a little more than unimpressed. It would be safe to say the light bringer would be absolutely furious.

"No, scrap that. Samuel would be seething. All his best laid plans to observe this creature that is seemingly doomed to the dark world gone to hell! He'd be so cross with me that I'd be better off flying out of there and never returning, that's for sure," Astrid murmured in a low voice.

Once again, he was doing his utmost to not get caught spying on Isra and of course the lowly human, Jonathan. Astrid kept his eye on the tall yet handsome mortal as he seemed to be in a close-up position. His body slanted sideways as he leaned across Isra, looking like he was about to kiss her.

Oh no, Astrid thought. *He better not attempt that. I don't want his grubby hands all over her. I can't comprehend the idea that his lips could be glued to hers. Oh no, he really better refrain from that nonsense!*

It was baffling to Astrid how he felt this way. He'd never even met Isra, never mind being close to her in the romantic sense. How was it that he felt so apprehensive over the idea that another man might be having his way with her? Astrid knew there was something special about this witch, but he hadn't anticipated that romantic feelings might come into play. This was strange to him, for he was a bird and she was seemingly human.

One might wonder how such a relationship could be feasible given the very real physical situation here. Astrid didn't even know how such a feminine figure like Isra would react to someone like him, never mind the fact he had silken black feathers and sharpened claws. That would be the most difficult aspect. But still, it was apparent from his jealousy over Jonathan wanting to kiss Isra that Astrid possessed some kind of feeling for the young witch. Just what would Samuel say on the subject? Astrid guessed he'd be mighty cross with him over it.

Hmm, I best keep this devotion to myself. At least for now, he thought to himself.

It was important not to be swayed by his emotions, for Isra was still his assigned task, if you will. And he needed to watch her unless he wanted to find another source of employment. Back to Jonathan. Now the mortal was really going for the gusto here. He leaned across Isra, their knees touching.

The thing Astrid couldn't figure out was whether the witch was comfortable with this arrangement, as she wasn't saying anything to Jonathan. She seemed shy in a funny sort of way, stiff as she inched away from Jonathan, almost at an angle, possibly so she could dart away at any given opportunity, perhaps?

As expected, the conversation between them was hardly anything to get into a lather about. Jonathan was laying on every ounce of immoral pizzazz he could muster on Isra. He was plausibly expecting her to fall over herself, bedazzled by his poetic wit, but that didn't seem to be so.

Jonathan leaned in a little closer to Isra, placing his elbow next to her very shaky knee. He tried to make it seem casual by holding a relaxed stance, but it was apparent he wanted to see what she would do. This caused Isra's eyebrow to rise alarmingly high as if she hadn't anticipated such a bold move from him. Jonathan was obviously very keen to pursue something with her, but her response was speaking the opposite of what Jonathan yearned for.

"You expected more for someone like me?" Jonathan asked her with a quizzical gaze, noting that her face was frozen, motionless and unsure of what to do.

Isra was evidently nervous and moved over just a tiny bit, away from Jonathan. It brought her closer to the end of the couch. However, it was so subtle that he barely noticed she had taken her distance.

"Yes, I expected something more prosperous for you. I mean, you come off as such a regal specimen," Isra explained, taking heed to stay where she was, keeping her eye on Jonathan just in case he had any ideas of getting closer to her.

"Specimen?" Astrid mocked. "Well, that's one word for him." Astrid huffed as he continued to look in on the two blossoming souls in love, or more accurately, just one soul in lust.

"Ah well. Riches are not something that come easily to everyone," Jonathan recounted with a distorted smile, swallowing a little as he resisted something inside himself, like the urge to vomit.

It wasn't something he enjoyed talking about since he had lost all claim to his father's throne, but it upset him greatly. Valien had always been considered the more worthy son and therefore the rightful prince. But for Jonathan to be stripped of his heritage completely, well he really resented that to the extent that Jonathan had no time for his father or for Valien for that matter, but Valien always invited Jonathan to fanciful balls and elaborate parties that went on into the wee night hours nonetheless.

Jonathan felt that attending these events was just a reminder of what he had lost. A fatal sting in the tail adding further shame and guilt to his rejection. It was an adorned and rather spiffy party that had led to him meeting the wonderfully shallow Everilda though. At least that was something. Or not, depending on how you judged knowing the vindictive and spiteful Everilda.

"I see," Isra stated, quickly changing her tone to avoid the subject completely as she felt she had made a faux pas in even challenging Jonathan about why he didn't have a better life or at least something to show for it.

"Anyway, that's not why you are here." Jonathan edged closer to her, looking into her eyes, meeting hers his own. He was so up close and personal with Isra that she could detect a faint whiff of the cinnamon tea on his breath that they had consumed only a few minutes ago.

If he got any closer, Isra might have fainted from the shock of not knowing how to compose herself in such a situation. She had imagined getting intimate with him, but probably not in the sense that he'd had in mind. Isra figured they would have a more intellectual connection based upon a mutual friendship of sharing one's secrets and so forth. Being physically abutting was not something she'd desired.

"Yes, why am I here? That is an interesting conundrum," Isra cooed, almost breathless from Jonathan being so adjacent to her.

If there was a way out of this awkward flabbergasted situation, Isra would be making a swift exit right about now. Being around Jonathan was intoxicating and yet exciting. It was the kind of relationship that one loved to hate, as cliché as it was.

Jonathan seemed to have lost some of his inner cool as now he appeared quite nervous being around Isra. Strange, as he had been so calm and collected before, almost seducing her with his body so meticulously close to her on-edge pristine figure. Perhaps it was the way she spoke so formally about her being here. Maybe this intimated Jonathan a little. He was used to having his way with women of all varieties. It was a shock to him that Isra was the first that wasn't exactly forthcoming to his advances. She was a whole different kettle of cinnamon tea than what he was used to.

Jonathan was just about to voice his manly speech on why Isra should succumb to him and surrender to his proposed courting when he became distracted by a shuffling sound on the window ledge. Bemused, Jonathan looked across at the window only to find a pair of yellow golden eyes meet his own and then disappear at a moment's notice as the raven darted from Jonathan's line of vision.

"Shit!" Astrid chirped quickly, darting around the corner only to grimace as he found himself next to a damp wall saturated in lime green mold.

How charming. He doesn't have good house decor and neither does he know how to keep things clean. Is there anything this mortal does excel at? Astrid thought with a huff, turning around in disgust. There was no way he was going to sit by that rancid wall, no matter what Samuel had insisted.

"That's twice in one sitting I've almost discovered. Good golly!" Astrid countered, shaking away some rank green mildew from his feathers. The raven was starting to feel like this mission to keep watch on the young, rebellious witch was proving too hot to handle. "Hmmm, perhaps I shall wait until he is distracted again," Astrid got closer to the window, attempting to peek his eyes at the scene in that dreary mortal's home.

It was amusing as Astrid saw that Jonathan looked so bewildered over the entire incident that if he kept on staring at that window ledge, he may just spontaneously combust. Of course, that would be a very generous outcome in Jonathan's case.

Jonathan was already distracted however, mulling over it in his mind. His darkened eyes darted back and forth to the window ledge and then to Isra again. But Isra, who also seemed confused as she eyed him with suspicion as if he was something to be extremely cautious of, looked at him with such revolt. It suggested that Isra thought that perhaps there was just something not quite right with Jonathan.

Jonathan, no matter how he tried, could not get the scenario out of his mind. The image of the raven ran riot in Jonathan's head, but this was strange to Jonathan because he'd only seen it for a second. Or less.

That was weird, Jonathan muttered to himself in thought, wondering if he had actually witnessed the raven or if he'd imagined the whole thing. *A raven?* Jonathan motioned quizzically to himself in thought. *Now what was one of those beings doing by my window ledge? I must be paranoid, as it looked like it was spying on me. No, that's presumptuous of me. Perhaps I am just too overwhelmed with anxiety because I am trying to be cool and casual in front of my lady friend.*

Obviously, Jonathan wasn't going to get any straight answers since he was rambling away to himself in silent chatter, but it did make him feel very peculiar all of a sudden. And less confident. The last thing he needed was a slump in feeling like he was the king of everything. Not that he ever would be a king in the physical sense, but you get my drift.

Oh, to merry hell with it! I'm just going to come out with it and tell her what I want for us. She either joins me or runs away leaving me chasing her back to that dreaded Wingdom's where dear old Everi also hails,

Jonathan said excitedly in thought as if he was giving himself a much needed pep talk.

Jonathan returned his attention back to Isra, almost having his manly body shifted right next to hers, and then he gave her his shiny smile, displaying a nice set of sparkling white teeth. And before anything else could jeopardize it, Jonathan bravely opened his mouth in sheer hope that Isra would entertain his idea of them cultivating their youth and going forth to new heights.

"So, I was wondering what you'd say to you and I courting?" Jonathan uttered as Isra went bright beet red.

"Courting?" Isra asked, seeming flustered. The pale porcelain skin tone she normally had was now as bright and beaming as a shiny red apple.

"Yes, for companionship. Becoming one part of a wholesome ... well...." He stopped mid-sentence, quickly losing his train of thought.

Jonathan realized he hadn't prepared himself for this onset of nerves that was attacking him. He felt the wind sweep through him as a wave of nausea rippled inside his stomach. He struggled to find the right words to make his request seem just. It seemed like Jonathan was already making a fine mess of this and he'd only just found the courage to ask her to be his, in a manner of speaking.

"I think I understand what you are trying to say," Isra interrupted him, softly meeting him in a joint glance where her emerald green eyes affixed onto his.

She didn't say anything for a moment neither did she take her eyes off him. For the first time in Isra's life she felt comfortable and confident around a man. A warm glow echoed around her in sweet hues of peach. Her aura practically danced at the sight of the handsome and yet beguiling Jonathan. A mint hue could be seen in the center of her eyes, normally where nothing but dark, shimmering emerald green could be found. This was really rather novel for someone who didn't often show any signs of emotive feeling.

Jonathan didn't say anything, but staying in the moment, he closely leaned in to Isra pulling her toward him into a huge bear hug that was viewed as quite masculine. He didn't want to go to the whole hog of planting a kiss on her lips. It had taken an awful lot of gusto for him just to get somewhere with her. There would be plenty of time for romance and lips someplace else.

While Isra was locked in the tight embrace with Jonathan, her eye suddenly darted across to the window again, but this time Astrid was quick to move out of sight, holding his breath as that green eye centered back on Jonathan again. After a second, Jonathan finally released her from his tight, manly grip.

It was then that Isra pondered the idea that there could be something in this. Some bright future filled with joy and love, delighting in the precipice that having a male companion would now present to her so many marvelous opportunities of which her life had only just begun. A small smile appeared on her porcelain face symbolizing the softness of the juncture.

This moment of Isra seeming so warm in nature was something to behold for the rugged raven who was watching the scene just quietly lurking beyond the window. He didn't want to get caught again so he had taken heed in placing himself just at the edge of the window sill where he could very swiftly duck out of any watchful eye view if deemed necessary.

Astrid quietly waltzed off into his own head as he recalled the instructions from Samuel to watch Isra for she was a major player in darkness. Astrid didn't understand that notion at all. He felt that the messengers from on high had made a huge mistake with this one. She didn't seem even remotely dark.

No way can this creature ever be dark, he murmured in thought to himself. *There is no logical reasoning for it. It's absolutely preposterous. I've sat and watched her and I can see nothing that suggests she may turn the tide. I don't see what all the fuss is about! But I suppose I should head back.*

And with that, Astrid lifted his wings, launching into the sky since he was anxious to get back to Samuel and confer with him over what he had witnessed. Isra, the witch in training, really didn't appear to be wicked at all, not in Astrid's eyes anyway.

9

The next morning, Isra was bubbly, feeling as if she was floating on air. The spring in her step was an even bigger indication of her joyful mood as she fluttered around Everilda's living space without a care.

However, the fair-haired witch smelled a rat because there was only one possible cause for Isra's lively disposition that she was demonstrating all of a sudden. Everilda's eyes glazed over Isra, carefully noting how Isra almost glided across the cold stone floor like she was dancing when she paraded around the kitchenette to make some tea.

Hmmm, if that isn't a sign of a girl in love, I cannot conceive what is! Everilda cursed through her teeth as her thoughts tore through her mind, adding to the anger she already felt. *That callous man has disobeyed me. Jonathan has gone behind my back despite my harsh warnings and decided to carry on this merry charade with our sweet little Isra. And now she's in a state of bliss completely unaware that I am a factor in her blooming romance. Oh, what is a girl to do when a man refuses to buckle down to reason? It was one simple order he was given, to drop Isra from his bosom and yet he has not surrendered to my will in doing that. Oh, how will I punish him for this? Hmmmm,* Everilda thought to herself in solemn silence.

"That man will get his comeuppance, sooner or later. I will see to that," Everilda mumbled as she sat cross-legged on the couch, still eyeballing Isra for more evidence that the girl was hopelessly in love.

How poignant, really. The girl meets Jonathan when I ditched her for some lothario who was so memorable I can't even recall the name of him, but not that it matters. Our Isra laid eyes on Jonathan and that was it. Sparks flew all across the wide open luscious spring green plains. And who could blame her? He is quite the catch, but he's mine. That man belongs to me. Sure, I don't love him or even want him, not when it comes down to it. But still, I own him.

"I must find a way to let him know that..." Everilda retorted sullenly while having her index finger positioned to the base of her lips.

"You must find a way to let him know what?" Isra interrupted. She stood before Everilda with a smile so beaming and brilliant white that it made Everilda wonder if it had the power to unleash flame just from the sheen of it.

Oh drat. I didn't plan on this happening. Be swift now, Evie. Find a way to throw her not exactly subtle nose far away from the stench of the beef sirloin before she catches on to just how rancid it really is.

And yet again Everilda was colliding amongst her own thoughts, torn between the idea of ripping Jonathan and Isra apart and also dealing with the wimpy, pathetic embodiment of a man.

"Oh, nothing dear," Everilda quickly cajoled in response.

Jeez, how quick did Everilda have to be with that one? Yes, it was true Isra was a little naïve, but she was definitely not stupid.

Isra sat down beside Everilda holding two steaming mugs of what smelled tart and bitter, perhaps resembling something a little bit chocolaty. One might possibly wonder just what was at the forefront of Isra's mind to come up with such a frightfully delicious concoction. Clearly the young witchlet was in fine spirits as she sat down beside Everilda after her brassy friend had gratefully taken the cup into her own hands. Everilda paused, sipping the dark brown liquid as she pursued the idea of questioning Isra further over the event.

Hmm, forget that. It could be viewed as cross examination and suppose our young Isra gets suspicious? No, I can't have that. I must work on Jonathan. That man sure as hell has a lot to answer for!

Isra stopped mid sip of her coffee. Her bright green eyes faced Everilda with a sweet but honest gaze, abruptly uttering, "Oh I can't stay long. I have a preexisting engagement. I hope you won't be bored too much by the drudgery."

Of course, Isra was referencing classes with Magnus Wingdom. Their dull and dreary head of coven was as exciting as a fart tinged with lemon. Not that farts were exciting, but just imagine a boring old man laced with bitterness, killing all the joy in your life. That was a fair enough summary of it.

Everilda spat her coffee right out of her mouth. The murky bitter beverage went everywhere, all over her crease-free black dress with lace edging at the hem and sleeves. And most importantly, all over Isra's dress as well. Isra was taken aback, quickly getting up to retrieve a cloth, wiping it down on her dress. Thankfully Isra was dressed all in black too so there would not be a stain, but Everilda's behavior was puzzling her.

"Is there something I said, Evie?" Isra asked, feeling somewhat cautious around her friend as if there might be a reason for her to be so ill tempered.

Everilda composed herself effortlessly as if she were just wiping some filthy matter away from her. Straightening herself on her footing, she made haste in darting over to the pot to gather a fresh cup of coffee, deliberately not allowing Isra to see her face for then she'd see what was really behind that spitting action.

"It's nothing. I'm just clumsy is all. So, pre existing engagement? I must know about this. Do sit here with me. Please glorify me with the details. I am sure to be impressed, I know." Everilda pressed, wondering if she had convinced herself that she was going to be all right knowing the truth of what was going on, never mind Isra. Although when she reflected back on it in an afterthought the whole, "I am sure to be impressed, I know" bit sounded rather sarcastic.

But then Everilda *was* pissed about the whole affair. It was obvious to all and sundry that Isra's secret rendezvous was going to be with Jonathan. No man had even come up close to the girl except that fiendish Jonathan, so he had to be the hot rod lighting the fire in young Isra's heart. There were no other candidates to fit the possibility unless our Isra was a dark horse and had the males of Seclera eating out of her hand.

But then again that would really be something, Everilda joked to herself in mid-thought.

Everilda discarded this quickly, reapplying a false smile on her irate face because let's face it, she couldn't have Isra being all curious and feeling like something wasn't quite right, could she?

Isra, on the other hand, remained stood up. Her footing was unsteady as if anxiety penetrated her being from head to toe. There was something eerie about the way she stood with her left foot a little more relaxed than the right one that indicated an uncomfortable sense of being within her.

"It's nothing, really," Isra lied as though she were trying to disregard the matter as unimportant. "It's just a dalliance with a stranger. Nothing more to tell," she added, further confirming Everilda's suspicions since Isra was being so vague about the whole affair.

"A dalliance, girl? I never even expected you to breathe the same air as a man. Much less hear of you being courted by one. Do tell me, who is it?" Everilda probed ever so gently.

Her voice sounded like honey that had been drenched in way too much syrup. She really had the gift of the gab when it came to being a pretentious fake temptress. Everilda could charm the pants off anything with her bogus, "I'm your best friend so tell me all," candy-coated manner when really she was doing all in her power to claim what she believed was rightfully hers. And woe betide anyone that just so happened to be an obstacle in Everi's path because she'd tear you down and not lose a second of sleep over it.

To be blunt, if Everilda truly thought that you had something that was worth her having but wasn't sure of how to attain it because you were being too secretive about it, she would morph into a softer version of herself, tapping into your emotions, finding your weak spot. Then she'd find the most strategic way to gain your trust, and once she was in...

Well, only a few know too well how that one ends up. And it isn't pretty.

One moment you have the picturesque life with white picket fence posts standing next to the man of your dreams, everything landing at your feet and the next, you're standing alone at that white fence, desolate and alone because our dear Everilda lured him with her wiles. And that would be the end of your fantastical life as you knew it right there. So quite frankly, it was best to not allow her to enter your world, mentally speaking, because that was where she did the most damage.

But Isra wasn't quite the same as most folk Everilda had torn down, ripping whatever love or companionship they had at the bitter seams, leaving nothing left to be salvaged. Isra was a bit unorthodox in her ways and yes, while she was innocent in the greater scheme of things, it probably wasn't going to be a very wise move to test the young witch. But Everilda wasn't bothered over something so mediocre.

"So, what of it?" Everilda pressed, sounding impatient because Isra wasn't exactly being forthcoming with the goods.

It had to be said that Everilda wasn't sure if she wanted to soak in every detail, but at the same time she needed to know what Jonathan was up to. So, she'd take the pain of hearing how he was parading Isra around him like some prized possession and then she'd deal with the matter as she saw fit.

"Ah, it's nothing, really Evie," Isra babbled. "It's just..."

She wandered off in thought before finishing the sentence, back in her little bubble again where everything was bright and drenched in rainbows, no doubt. Golly, how Everilda hated it when Isra did that. It was becoming vexing to Everilda that Isra was being so ambiguous over this tryst with Jonathan. And with Isra so close to spilling the beans, it was getting damn annoying that she was meandering into yet another transfixed state of oblivion.

Bloody typical of the girl, Everilda snarled to herself with it sounding like venom was dripping from her pursed lips. It almost felt like her frustration may well just burst out into the atmosphere, one that was already filled with much rawness. *Just spit it out, woman. Goodness!* Everilda said devilishly in thought, taking care to make sure she didn't express her wrath out loud because she couldn't have her nice-as-pie act exposed now, could she?

"It's what, dear?" Everilda asked again, feeling like they were rolling around in circles getting nowhere.

"I'm not sure," Isra gushed. "I mean, I like him and all. He's a handsome, fine structure of a man but I'm not sure if it's ... you know, meant for me." She twirled a strand of chocolate-brown hair around her finger clearly in a very nervous disposition.

She could have uttered that she didn't want this conversation at all but her body language in the way she stood so unnerved by the kitchenette area said it all. One could suppose that Isra could muster up the excuse to concoct another bitter and dark caffeinated beverage, but she wasn't in the frame of mind to think of it.

"Oh to merry hell with all that. Who cares if something doesn't feel like it's aimed in your direction? Girl, you only live this life once. You can't go around twiddling your thumbs and sheltering yourself away from all and sundry for all eternity. You never know what you might miss!" Everilda delivered in a strict tone as if she was unleashing a torrid reprimand for Isra.

"Well, perhaps you are right, Evie," Isra relented, inching toward the iron kettle that was lying discarded on the stove. Without thinking about it, Isra touched the kettle just ever so gently with the tip of her index finger only to find an involuntary pang as her skin was branded by the iron appliance.

"Ouch!" Isra squealed, shaking her finger in hopes it would quell the pain. She pulled back a little, turning her face sideways in the direction of Everilda.

The fair-haired witch sat on the couch acknowledging Isra's glance with a coarse look signifying how painfully annoyed she was before even harsher words slid out of her mouth like molten lava.

"Yes, my dear, you will get burned by things that are not meant for you. That vile burning sensation you feel broiling your skin is acting as a deterrent thus ensuring that you stay away," Everilda retorted callously. Her voice sounded as though acid were bubbling away down her throat.

"I see that..." Isra rambled almost incoherent as she tended to her burnt finger.

Isra felt conflicted. She didn't know whether this well-chosen array of words was a threat or not. It sounded menacing in its manner. The way Everilda spoke was chilling like ice spilling down her veins replacing her rich, lustrous blood. But there was no solid confirmation as to what Everilda meant, as she was keeping her meaning obscured.

This was a deliberate act on Everilda's part; she could be very indistinct with the way she conveyed her thoughts.

The way it was with Everilda, well she was a tricky character indeed to say the least. She'd go off on a tangent, metaphorically speaking, leaving things on the stove and allowing them to simmer, but she'd never leave them on there long enough to finish boiling. That was Everilda in a snap. You'd never get to what was really going on. It was always par-boiled. Probably why nobody in her life could ever really work her out. She'd always leave things half baked, especially the truth, so it was no surprise that Isra couldn't figure out Everilda's motives with this supposed sinister threat that had come out of nowhere.

"Well, it's not something to get flustered about, dear. So, this young man of yours, what is he like? Do I happen to know him?" Everilda continued, abruptly changing the subject and becoming judge, jury, and executioner in the same breath.

"I don't think so," Isra answered, sounding hesitant as the shakiness echoed in her voice.

"He's not from around here then?" Everilda cut in abruptly.

The atmosphere between her and Isra was heating up with Everilda feeling more and angrier, but she had to keep up the facade. She needed to get to the truth even if she had to drag Isra by her hair in order to attain it.

"Eh? Oh, er, no," Isra replied quickly, stumbling upon her words. She was losing the ability to keep up with the white lies she was bursting out with. Or should we say, slightly tinged black ones?

But why did Isra feel so weird about telling Everilda the true identity of her mystery man? Was it that somewhere deep inside herself Isra did not really trust Everilda? They were friends, were they not? A dynamic duo whereby just being in the presence of these feisty young ladies sent chills out in every facet of Wingdom's coven, making the other witches in the academy look unbelievably boring in comparison. And of course, making them seem as though they lacked experience because Isra and Everilda already knew a lot about the magical arts long before they had set foot in the coven.

Even Magnus Wingdom had already given Everilda and Isra a good old talking to because of their reckless behavior, as well as a sheer telling off for their mutual lack of respect toward him even if he was a dim-brained old fool. Of course, they had actually shouted it out, making him red with embarrassment, all of this while lessons were in full swing.

Yes, it was fair to say the coven leader wasn't best pleased with Isra and Everilda. Not that the young witches gave a shit, you understand. They were far too busy laughing their heads off about every silly little thing.

It only made it even more bemusing as to why Isra was being so closed off with Everilda now.

"I feel like there is something you are not telling me, dear," Everilda chided in Isra's direction. Her fierce veracity was brewing in the form of unkempt anger that was building up to its ultimate climax. Realistically it could implode at any given moment, especially if Isra kept on being so elusive with the truth.

For goodness sake girl, just tell me it's Jonathan. I already know it is him. I know with every fiber of my being that he is the one setting your heart aflutter. It's no quarrel, not really. But you can't have him. He's my plaything. My little toy of which I can yank his strings whenever I desire, Everilda growled to herself in thought as if she was actually speaking it to Isra, when in fact she was just thinking it.

"Oh, it's nothing," Isra muttered, brushing it off. "I have to go or else I will be late," she added as an elaborate excuse.

"Have a splendid evening, but remember about these sensual desires over things that are not meant for you, dear," Everilda hushed her with a drawn out tone demonstrating how ticked off she was. A cryptic coming together that could only spell out trouble indeed.

10

Isra turned to Jonathan with a formidable gaze. She had been here with him for almost an hour now, but something seemed wrong. She couldn't put her finger on it. He was just so iffy with her. Distant. Almost as though he didn't want to be there but yet he'd gone to the effort of arranging this little rendezvous.

And it was no surprise that their location was none other than his little cottage in between Spirisity and Seclera where not a soul could disturb them. Or maybe someone would!

Still, despite the engineered privacy that had been so elaborately laid out, Isra smelled a rat and she wanted to pull Jonathan up about it. It was so weird. The line of questioning Everilda had taken earlier with her was making her quiver. So many ambiguous phrases had exploded from Everilda's mouth as if she was hinting at something. It was intoxicating just being around her best friend and that was a bold thing for Isra to say, but she felt it so deeply in her soul. Something was just terribly wrong there.

And it wasn't just with their "friendship" but the way Everilda behaved around Isra lately. How she kept on uttering out unknown phrases that Isra couldn't and maybe also didn't want to understand. Seeing her best friend transform so dramatically that she wondered if

65

Evie was even inside there anymore was quite peculiar for Isra. Who would know?

Anyway, for now at least, Isra could have a break from all that. Being out here in the middle of nowhere with Jonathan would be satisfying enough to calm her over chattering mind. Isra was going to get to the heart of the matter whether Jonathan consented to her doing so or not. Finally, after what seemed like a century of staring into his bold brown eyes, Isra plucked up the courage to ask him what she had been dreading knowing the truth of.

"If I asked you something, would you be honest with me?" she requested to him. Silence was the only thing that followed. Isra felt a sharp pang in her heart, fearing the worst.

"I ... I ... I am sorry," Jonathan sputtered, turning his head away as he was unable to face her.

Oh golly, look at that, she mused in her thoughts as she watched Jonathan's unmistakable reaction.

Well, it was no surprise really, was it? The man practically recoiled. His eyes darkened as he backed away from Isra which was impossible as they were sitting next to one another, just on the grassy bank that wasn't too far away from his home.

This can't be good, Isra said to herself in her mind.

The impending anxiety felt like it was about to have its wicked way with her. Now Isra stopped in a trance. In the midst of the quiet, Isra began to connect Jonathan's reaction to something Everilda had said earlier on.

Everilda had barely said two words to Isra back in her room earlier, but the things she had mentioned screamed volumes like a banshee crying out, ushering in the echo that would follow a soul before its life was to be cruelly taken. Everilda's shadowy and undignified mannerisms had only added to Isra's growing suspicions.

Everilda should have just produced an old, tattered book covered in inelegible writing and given it to Isra, willing her to translate it. But instead, she chose to spout out meaningless words that gave no clue to their meaning.

Glaring at Jonathan, almost seething with rage at him for not answering her, Isra turned her focus to the luscious spring green hills just ahead of where she was sat. The tall, majestic hills gave the illusion that they ascended right up to the very top of the cloudless skies. Everything up there looked so tiny when you stared up at it from the bottom of this end of the earth. The rich green hills dominated the land above but nobody even knew what one would find over the radiant hills because they appeared too high for one to reach. Not to mention the golden matter that shined within those Masonic stone walls. But the land of Spirisity was a mere legend to the citizens that dwelled between it and Seclera.

And if the "on high," the light bringers, had their way it would remain so. They simply couldn't allow any cross contamination between the realms. That really wouldn't go down well with their boss, Samuel.

Isra, completely unaware of any of that, considered the idea that Jonathan was being reticent because he was guilty of some atrocity. He seemed terribly troubled over her question and yet he did not have the courage to give her a response. It was beginning to seem like Jonathan and Everilda's actions were slowly being tied together, connecting up as one. The picture suddenly became more and more apparent that somehow their actions could be linked.

Of course, if you had suggested the idea to Isra that Jonathan and Everilda were aligned in more ways than one, she would have shrugged it off, labeling it as outrageous. However, she was now thinking of the likelihood of it.

But it's impossible. They aren't even acquainted with each other. It's preposterous! It's insane! Isra went as far to say in her cycle of thought.

Isra barely took notice as a raven quietly entered in on the scene, taking its position behind her on the crumbling roof of Jonathan's cottage.

～

THE FUNNY THING was Astrid the raven wasn't surprised by Isra's explosive mind revolt.

Yes, it was true. Astrid wasn't just any old raven. He had the ability to read thoughts of both humans and animals alike. Why else did he have the job of keeping his beady eye on Isra, heralded by the chief light bringer in the land, Samuel? It wasn't because of his dashing personality, that was for sure.

"Oh please! He's going to do that. The weak, pathetic piece of skin he is. The man is guilty as sin, girl! Don't you know anything? Do I have to fill in the blanks of what is occurring here?" Astrid charged in behind her. "Oh shit, she's not supposed to have knowledge of my being here. Scrap that."

He remembered he was here on a reconnaissance mission specifically to spy on Isra, checking for any signs she might turn the tide heading into her supposed darkness. To be truthful, Astrid didn't even believe that Isra was going to go down that path. She seemed in good spirits for someone of the mere age of seventeen. As far as he could observe she didn't have any of the classic traits that a human being would display before they were to descend into the somber reality, he knew all too well.

Actually, Isra did have one of those key attributes: this Jonathan character. This pesky human seemed to be in the young witch's bosom. This man seemed to be at the forefront of Isra's mind every second she took a breath. But goodness knows why. It's not like he was caring or interested in her emotional being. Just another prissy snob that had lost out on claiming the kingdom. Pathetic state of a man, really.

Yeah, Astrid didn't give a shit. He told it like he saw it. No point smothering something really gross in lashings of chocolate now, was there? Unless you really wanted your luscious, sweet offerings saturated in layers of filth that were soon to show their true colors as you bit into their flesh. But by all means, go ahead if you like that. I'll pass, thanks.

But Astrid saw this romancing technique quite a lot so it wasn't uncommon. These so-called gentlemen would seek out a girl like Isra and then taint her by robbing their virginity, taking away what made them sweet and then when the damage was done, they'd run a mile and never return.

Astrid did not like Jonathan. There was just a commodity that smelled so iffy about the mortal. He could not figure out why the man was so irritating to him. Maybe it was the way he did his utmost to weasel his way out of every mess he'd got himself into. Or maybe it was the lies that never ceased to end. Astrid didn't know. He didn't want to spend too much time thinking about it since there was a job to do here. Keep an eye on Isra. Help her if he could. And hopefully be there to provide some assistance against the raging hellfire if she did indeed go dark.

But I suspect there will be more than blasting flames if she does indeed succumb to that way of living, Astrid murmured in thought.

Anyway, time was getting on. It was almost nightfall. If this mortal and Isra were going to have any more interaction worth watching it was likely it wouldn't be tonight. Humans always liked to be in their beds before the harsh cover of night descended upon the realm. Astrid knew this was factual based on his frequent dealings with humans. They feared it when the sun went down for some reason, but maybe it was due to the fact that night was when the real inhabitants of the land came into themselves. You know, the witches, fairies, and other gross creatures we won't mention.

And on the subject of twilight, it was time for Astrid to report back to his boss, Samuel, on what he had witnessed today. Astrid was sure that Samuel would be delighted to know of the charming human being that was in Isra's midst, or perhaps not.

11

Samuel was sitting in the dark with just a tiny bit of light emitting from a cream-colored candle carefully laid out on the window ledge beside him. Samuel was clearly occupied this evening. His eyes were affixed to a large book that was positioned in front of him, staring absent-mindedly at the pages as if he was somewhere else.

With his faithful servant and friend Astrid off gallivanting and keeping an eye on the witch that was prone to darkness, Samuel had decided on some quiet time to read and reflect. Not that he didn't have time to read. Samuel was the chief of the light bringers that Isra would later come to affectionately refer to as "the love and light brigade," but Samuel's job was more delegating and communicating with the beings of the metaphysical realm. He did not actually physically do anything, but sometimes he would personally attend certain situations where dark was involved just to give it that special touch.

It was also why Samuel had servants like Astrid off doing the stalking, or should we say spying, on those that the "on high" stated were prime targets to turn over to the wicked and sinister side of life because Samuel stayed within his homely gray walls dishing out orders. And let's face it; he excelled at doing that.

Samuel continued to pore over the pages of his book when suddenly he was distracted by a large crash, almost making him jump out of his red velvet armchair as he turned his head to the window. Curious as to who or what this was, Samuel adjusted his silver half-moon glasses and was awestruck at what he saw. Upon further inspection of the incident, Samuel noticed his cream candle had been blown out, leaving melted creamy wax all over the place.

Well, that is going to be a fine mess to clean up, Samuel cursed to himself in annoyance.

Samuel didn't pay attention. He was busy surveying the lumps of wax that were quickly hardening all over his precious window ledge. But if he had, he'd have seen the thing that had caused the commotion was none other than Astrid.

"I'm sorry, Master. Awkward landing. I must do more to prevent that!" Astrid excused himself, shaking the dirt from his feathers.

Astrid's head was bowed downward as if in a defensive stance. He was nothing but apologetic, seeming to be very embarrassed over the rumpus he had caused. Astrid should have known better than to attempt flying in an open window. But he had not seen the lit candle. He was lucky just to have snuffed the thing out with himself because he could have scorched his feathers. Fire and feathers were not a very good combination.

Yes, I'll note that for future reference. Astrid sighed. *Look for bright orange flame before flying into open windows unless you want to set yourself alight. Luckily on this occasion that did not happen, but next time I may not be so fortunate.*

He was all in a flapper with himself, looking down at the window ledge, feeling out of sorts as he couldn't even look his master in the eye for fear of what might happen. For all Astrid knew, Samuel could have been very cross.

"Yes, well, don't worry yourself over it. Solid wax is fortunately easy to peel off the toughest of surfaces," Samuel coaxed. "Just be more careful next time," he added, still noting that Astrid's demeanor wasn't how he usually presented himself.

Astrid still appeared to be irritated and also annoyed like he had been around someone or something that had really rifled his feathers. Presumably that piece of junk Jonathan, but Samuel wasn't aware of the mortal's existence, not yet.

"Anyway, let's not waste any time in getting down to it. I want to know every single thing you saw of our lovely witch today, Astrid," Samuel remarked with a casual grin.

Lovely witch? Is he being sarcastic? Astrid mused sardonically in thought.

Samuel could be very quick witted when it came to a good insult. Even if he gave the impression that he was being dignified with you, he could throw in a snappy phrase that would have you questioning the entirety of what he said. Astrid swallowed a little. Ah yes, the inquisition. Samuel was going to ask about this sooner or later, but would Astrid have the courage to tell him everything he caught sight of today?

"Yes, Samuel," he acknowledged.

Astrid paused, thinking for a moment of what he was going to relay over Samuel. Some of the things he had learned while spying on Isra were valuable knowledge and Astrid wasn't sure how Samuel would take some not so pleasant things he had observed being the fore focus of Isra's life.

"Well, the witch Isra is a very interesting character. I have seen that she is a young, innocent soul. But..." Astrid stopped, quickly realizing he was about to blow the water out of the ocean where Jonathan was concerned.

Oh shit, I hadn't meant to get to that fine detail yet. Damn that mortal! Astrid cursed to himself.

Samuel noticed Astrid stalling. Samuel twiddled his fingers in a rhythmic motion, getting impatient with Astrid's tiresome delivery. "Yes, Astrid. But what? Is there something that the on high failed to mention?" Samuel inquired with a furrowed brow matched with his stern gaze. The kind of stare that burned right into you and knew right away if you were telling him a wild tale.

Astrid hesitated in answering Samuel. The sheer yellow sheen of his eyes was a little brighter in this touch of pitch black serenity as he mulled over everything he had discovered so far about Isra.

"It's nothing that bears any terrible importance," Astrid alleged.

Well, that was untrue. Because a mortal in the presence of the witch doomed to go downhill was of huge precedence. If anything, it was only adding weight to Isra's supposed impending cataclysm.

Samuel twitched his eyebrow immediately, clicking his index finger to his thumb in an almost violent action. "Oh no, you can do better than that, Astrid. Come on now, don't be a peasant. You know I don't have much liking for them," Samuel barked with a gruffness in his voice.

He really didn't have much of a fancy for peasants, but goodness knows why. However, Astrid wasn't one of those flighty bumpkins, but the look Samuel was flashing at him wasn't giving the raven confidence that Samuel was having much of an affinity for him either. Uh oh. That harsh glare was all it took. It would have been stupendous for Astrid to leave out anything because the last thing you'd want to do was get Samuel mad.

"Yes, you are right, Master," Astrid coughed, fighting away his nervousness. "I have witnessed something I did find particularly unappealing. There is a man in the witch's midst. A human," Astrid concluded, allowing Samuel to soak in this newly received information.

At first, Samuel said nothing, merely putting a finger to his lip as if in thought over something but he was so enigmatic with it you couldn't fathom just what he was contemplating. It took him a good minute or so before he gave Astrid a response.

"Go on," Samuel urged, saying nothing more. It was as though Samuel were digesting everything Astrid had relayed so far but now he needed the full story from Astrid in order to proceed.

"The man is not a very nice fellow. He's rather egotistical. He has the perception that he's the be all and end all. He fancies himself quite a bit," Astrid chirped.

"Does he now?" Samuel mused in a comical tone as if he found it entertaining.

"Yes. I detest him, if I am honest," Astrid concurred almost a little too eagerly.

"And so you should be! Especially in my presence," Samuel asserted.

Oh my, was there really any pleasing the man who took care of everything that was light and good? Samuel was really on one. Astrid couldn't quite tell just what had got into him this evening. Maybe it was him crashing into Samuel's pristine establishment and sending hot wax all over the place when he made his entrance? *Must remember to look where I am going before I land for future reference. For although Samuel is my master and dear friend, I cannot test his patience by being so insolent,* Astrid noted in his thoughts.

"Always, Samuel," Astrid agreed.

"Well, does this vagrant specimen of a human have a name?" Samuel demanded in a less hoarse tone although he still sounded rather brash.

"He does indeed. He goes by Jonathan in the human world," Astrid confirmed.

"Jonathan who? Does the man have a last name or a history? A heritage of some interest that might tickle the fancy of the on high?" Samuel insinuated as he continued to pick Astrid's brain on the matter.

"He is Prince Valien's brother," Astrid answered in a calm manner. "King Marco decided that his son Jonathan was not worthy of the throne due to his misgivings and not so charming behavior. And so the crown fell to Valien leaving Jonathan in a rundown cottage with only the glory of his name," Astrid recalled in detail.

"Oh, I see it for what it is now. This prissy little prick fancies himself as a king but the reality is he's living in delirium," Samuel chortled with glee.

"Yes," Astrid declared.

Samuel said nothing for a moment with only a smug smile affixed to his face as if one was in hysterics over something profoundly amusing. One could only wonder what hilarity was occurring in the crevice of Samuel's mind.

"Keep a firm eye on him. I want a full report on everything he does. Every person he encounters and the conversations he has, especially with our witch in question," Samuel ordered, although he was sounding slightly more relaxed now.

"Yes, absolutely, sir," Astrid piped up ardent as always.

Astrid paused because although this had been quite the interrogation, him having been questioned over everything he had observed from Isra and the not so regal Jonathan, there was something that was puzzling Astrid and utterly had been for several years now. But did he have the nerve to ask? It was so compelling that Astrid felt he had to know, although it could be seen as a breach of policies.

Oh, to hell with it! I've put up with worse from him, I'm just going to plunder in there and come out with it. The worst thing that can come my way is a severe telling off, Astrid chuckled to himself with mild amusement in his thoughts. He cleared his throat, feeling a tad nervous before delving into the mysterious realm that he was about to nose-dive into.

"Samuel, while I don't wish to impose on your business, I am curious as to why you don't like peasants? I mean, why do they bother you so much?" Astrid asked bravely as his bold yellow eyes met Samuel's in an intense moment.

For a brief second, Astrid wasn't sure if he'd made a grave mistake since Samuel was emotionless, barely even twitching. The air between them was tense as a tiny bit of the nightly wind sweeping in was the only softness in the room.

"Astrid, I would hate to think that you are poking your beak into places it does not belong! I just don't like peasants. I refuse to elaborate on such matters," Samuel informed him with a cold riveting glare.

Astrid didn't have much further to add to this statement, only nodding and bowing his head down as if in great shame. *Oops, I pushed him too far. Well, I was curious. I mean, they're only people, so why doesn't he find them endearing? There must be some reasoning for it,* Astrid jabbered away in thought, looking up suddenly and fearing he had been heard as Samuel continued to stare at him in a most hard-boiled manner.

"Don't you have a witch to spy on?" Samuel pressed, seeming irritated all of a sudden.

"Yes. I do," Astrid acknowledged.

"Good. Off with you then!" was all that came of Samuel's mouth as Astrid took the hint that it was the perfect time to take flight in the arms of the midnight blushed skies.

12

"Yes, that was a most pleasant conversation, wasn't it? Absolutely splendid, one must say," Astrid muttered to himself in the midst of his flight as he hovered above the stately Wingdom's Academy.

After the awkward discussion that had commenced between himself and Samuel earlier on, Astrid had decided upon something a little bit different on this night. It still revolved around keeping watch on Isra of course, but he had a slightly more ingenious tactic in mind. So far Astrid had only spied on Isra via neutral territory, but now he wanted to witness how she appeared in a more relaxed atmosphere. Naturally her residential quarters at Wingdom's were the best choice.

"So much to do and in so little time," Astrid continued as he coursed around the never-ending spindling gray towers of Wingdom's wondering just which one he'd discover Isra in.

Of course, it was like searching for a needle in a haystack as there were at least four neighboring sullen gray tall towers all sticking out into those intoxicating blackened skies. And with the cheery shade of light having long been discarded, it would be even more difficult to distinguish which one of those many black iron framed windows would be Isra's.

There were so many tiny oval shaped windows standing out in their jet-black coloring descending down the gray towers one by one like dainty dots. It would propose an interesting challenge sourcing out the one that Isra dwelled in, but let's not forget Astrid had remarkable gifts beyond many human expectations. He could find her by metaphysically sensing her energy. Almost like the same way he prowled her usually, but using the essence of her, the part of Isra that made her what she was: her soul. When you took stock of the issue at hand, this really was the most likely solution that would prove to be successful.

Astrid knew from experience that there was a surefire way to seek out a witch at any time whether it was dusk or just after midnight and that was by connecting to her in the most profound way, by reaching into her heart, mind and soul, finding all the aspects that made a witch what they were. Astrid hoped it wasn't too late for him to find Isra's heart space and tune into that energy. He had witnessed some iffy things around her lately that he did not approve of. Yes, the callous way Jonathan had been acting with her, not answering her when she had asked him if he was true to her.

It was saddening for the raven to see Isra being mistreated in this manner. It hurt him a lot because he saw a sweet, kind soul deep within the refusal to need anyone and the standoffish attitude that she maintained around nearly every single being she encountered. Astrid truly believed that Isra was worth saving. That there was a reprieve away from darkness. She didn't have to succumb to that terrible fate. She did have a choice. That was the bottom line, one he solely believed with every fiber of his spirit. But so far Astrid was the only one who seemed to be convinced that Isra was not a completely lost cause.

The night winds howled behind him sending out their rage ripping across the grassy banks that dominated the prestigious Wingdom's academy. Tonight was a turbulent night indeed with trees shaking their branches and violently batting against the terrain in the boisterous conditions.

I picked a fine old time to connect to her, didn't I? Astrid said to himself in thought.

Astrid realized he wasn't really in a position to connect to Isra so it was time to make a swift landing. But it wasn't exactly pleasant terrain having felt the rain drip down onto his sleek black feathers.

"Oh, I'm getting soaked. Now what? Where can one perch themselves where they will not be disturbed on this blustery night?!" he asked himself.

Looking down onto the land before him, he saw that there wasn't much in the way of a shelter except the famous cherry tree that could provide some warmth although it was likely he'd probably still get wet in some parts.

Hmm, where can I go? There must be somewhere that I can swoop down to and find a nice spot of which to converse with the realms, he queried himself in thought.

So yes, there was the option of the cherry tree, but as Astrid found himself just above the entrancing trunk he noticed that among the branches was a thick lime green mildew that was very wet and slimy, and also upon the branches was burgundy-red over ripened cherries, neither of which was appealing.

"All I want is a nice, dormant location. How hard can it be?" Astrid complained. He was clearly frustrated, for this search was proving to be more complex than he'd imagined.

And so Astrid continued looking for a place to go despite the rough climate that he was subjected to. The already rough winds began surging upon the land, leaving a trace on everything they touched, leaving nothing still. All the leaves were ripped away from the trees in a gusty spell as the wind gathered its force letting everyone know of its presence.

"Ah, now this Wingdom's Academy might prove fruitful. Yes, I know it is rather rude for someone to come to a place uninvited, but it is the small hours. I am sure nobody would notice if I just slipped in for a moment."

And with that, Astrid took a keen eye launching himself downward until he landed softly. With a quick shake of his feathers to get the rain out Astrid strode up the gray steps that led to that majestic ochre brown oak door, the entrance to where all the magic inevitably would happen. For such a provident place where they would deem to teach young witches the ways of magics, it seemed a little out of sorts. Astrid would have expected something a little more on the gothic side of things, but no matter. Not everyone has it down to a fine art when it comes to decor.

So off Astrid went over to the majestic oak door with its gold gilding making it shine in the night's barely there moon glow. Gearing himself up to it as he pushed past the solid wooden entity, he was surprised as it flew open. Now he took haste to be quiet for he was not meant to be in here, hoping with all his might that as he let the door shut behind him, it would not make too much of a clatter.

Ah, so here it was, the fine old establishment. Wingdom's Academy. The home to many young witches that came here from all of the lands wanting to become better acquainted with their skills in witchery and the not so forbidden arts. Of course, no doubt the darker stuff would not be taught to these ladies, so expect disappointment there.

Still looking over the grand hallway, it really was a sight to behold. A lush royal purple carpet elongated across the hall only to be mismatched by the light peach hue with golden shimmer that was painted across the walls.

Okay, maybe they do have good taste in decorating after all! Astrid agreed to himself. *So now where was I going? Remember, I need a quiet area in which to think and concentrate ... needs to be somewhere vacant. Ideally, a nice little corner in which one can hide in.*

Astrid glanced across the area around him. Only to notice to his left there was an open doorway with which there was a bold red curtain the shade of blood. In a hurry, Astrid pushed past the curtain only to find a simple room with just a purple velvet armchair covered with gold tassels at the arms. There was literally nothing else in the room except a large square window indicating that the rain was still hammering down across the land as it smacked against the glass pane repeatedly.

"Yes, well, that won't be bothering me. I am more concerned with getting wet," Astrid articulated, staring out at the fierce weather that would be forced upon him when he was done here.

With no need to search further, Astrid traipsed over to the purple armchair, setting himself down in the center of it.

"Perfect." He grinned, clearly pleased with himself on an expedition well done.

Now onto the real task at hand. Astrid closed his eyes while still sat in the chair, breathing slowly to gain his focus, softly concentrating on Isra, imagining her stood there right in front of him dressed in a long-sleeved lace black gown with her long chocolate-brown hair dangling down across her forehead almost getting in the way of her emerald green eyes. Her gown clung to the floor as it almost towered over her.

Come on now, let's get it together, Astrid motioned to himself in quiet thought as he found himself going off into a trance.

Suddenly feeling relaxed and like everything else around him was fading away, images softly began popping in and out of the corner of his mind's eye. They were blurry and not really in focus and withering by in a flash before he could notice what they were of. Still, they weren't Isra, so Astrid figured these visuals were not of great importance.

But he continued allowing this imagery to flow in and out, hoping that something would stick out soon and he would have arrived at his chosen destination: Isra's core. The heart of her. The place one could only reach by connecting to her spirit. The energy that surrounded her person, not the physical body that she currently inhabited. It took a second or two but at last, something had emerged. Oh, but what was it? He couldn't quite fathom what it was, but something was peeling away at the seams of Astrid's vision to reveal more of it.

Aha! Yes. That's it. Astrid's eyes lit up at once as finally he caught a glimpse of Isra in his mind's eye. The part one sees in when they are attuned to that of the supernatural. The key he held that could open the door to the wondrous and mystical elements of life.

Isra was almost unrecognizable in Astrid's vision. She was

standing before him dressed head to toe in the most elegant baby pink. The darkness of her emerald green eyes merged beautifully with the soft fragrant pink coloring, however there was more. Just above Isra's head was a golden archway made entirely of gold bricks and right at the top of the archway was barely legible writing that spelled out a sentence of some kind. "Isra, she who realms in the dark."

Astrid could hardly read it as the scrawl was so tiny, but he pushed himself to focus more on the fantastical vision, yearning to know what it said pertaining to Isra. After a moment, his intuitive eye resided on the gold archway again, but he also noticed Isra's physical stance had changed. She wasn't standing before the archway like she was previously. Now she was sitting down, almost cradling her entire body with her head bent. She appeared to be weeping. Her enchanting emerald green eyes shone out amidst the clutter that surrounded them. Astrid veered in closer to the visual of Isra, now observing her eyes were soaked with tears colliding down her pale porcelain face. So much hurt resided in this once bright and happy soul.

Ugh, I got sidetracked. I need to see the writing. I want to read what it says about her, Astrid murmured to himself in thought, annoyed with himself that he had allowed himself to be swayed by Isra's poignant glare. *Okay, focus now, Astrid.* His metaphysical eye veered up to the center of the archway to get a good view of the scrawl that was etched on to it. It would really be amazing to Astrid if anyone could manage to make out what was written there, but he was going to give it his all.

Finally, he zoned in on the cursive lettering, hovering over every syllable to not allow for any mistakes because it was imperative at this point to ensure he read it correctly. Astrid began mentally concentrating as he read over it, letter by letter. "Lady Isra, she who dwells in the dark. She who is destined to become the enchantress after love tears out her heart. She who will fall peril to the charms of a simple fragrant entity. May she reign in hell. All hail Lady Isra of the Dark."

Astrid stopped reading the elegant scrawl, now having digested it fully.

So that's it then. The prophecy. It must be the exact same one the "on high" were being so cryptic about, but here I discover it in the midst of another dimension, although I feel I was not supposed to learn about this yet, Astrid cautioned himself in thought as he continued musing over the much anticipated prophecy. *And I found it only because I chose to see her at the heart of who she was. I wonder if I will be scolded for going against Samuel's ways in reference to this? But he did practically tell me to get out of there, having been so irritated by my presence!*

"Oh well, it does not matter then. I simply will not mention it," Astrid commented quietly. "But alas, Samuel will ask me. Oh, to hell with it! It's not the first time I have told a blatant lie to my old friend and master," Astrid confirmed with a wistful grin. "He cannot be harmed by what he does not have the knowledge of. Ah well, that was refreshing to the mind to say the least."

Astrid opened his eyes. He gaped across at the window. The night was still raining on. A storm was ahead by the look of those gray skies saturated in molten gray clouds dominating one another mercilessly without a care. At any moment those heavens could open up and unleash fury and malice in the form of silvery white lightning cast out from the perilous skies.

"I better make a move. I am not supposed to be in here, after all," Astrid pointed out to himself.

Well, he was inside the grand Wingdom's Academy, Isra's place of scholarly learning, and he had not even been asked to be here. If someone was to discover him now, there could be serious questions and worse repercussions if Samuel found out.

"Yes, I can't imagine Samuel would be overjoyed if he knew about this. Best if I make a quick getaway now before someone sees me," Astrid concurred, swooping down onto the floor, maneuvering himself past the blood red curtain as quickly as he had entered.

Making haste now, he rushed down the royal purple flooring using his right claw to latch onto the door, bolstering it ajar so it was open enough for him to slip out. And he was about to do just that when he was distracted by a not so familiar voice.

"Jonathan! Don't you turn away from me!"

It was a female voice shouting in a harsh, aggravated tone. But it was not Isra evidently, because there was no softness anywhere to be found. And Astrid knew what Isra sounded like.

Hang on, why were they shouting at Jonathan? Oh, this can't be good! Astrid speculated, suddenly connecting the dots as to who that Jonathan could be. But he was wholeheartedly wishing that he would be proved wrong.

It was coming from outside, the shouting. So, Astrid allowed the door to shut behind him, being quick to hide himself around the corner of the gray steps as he would be witness to this showdown that was evidently occurring in these so called quiet hours.

"It's funny they don't say much while the sun is awake and cheering, but yet as soon as night comes in they are out there brash and brawling like dogs on a full moon," Astrid snickered quietly to himself, taking care to make sure he wasn't observed.

He took sight of the female in question that was doing all the screaming and cussing at this Jonathan character, whoever he'd turn out to be. Astrid stood taken aback as a fair-haired girl stood out amongst the moon's glow. Unlike Isra, she was a little shorter by say an inch and had blue eyes that glittered like sapphires in the twilight. She was definitely not Isra at all. Not by a long shot.

And by no surprise, the tall, dark-haired figure in the distance that she was yelling at looked up at her with bold chestnut eyes deep and penetrating as he gazed at her as if he wished to gain her approval, a bit like a dog who begged for scraps long before the meal was finished.

"Everi, do we have to do this? I mean ... here!" Jonathan glanced nervously at the majestic Wingdom's Academy, his eyes darting back and forth over the gray building.

"Oh please, like now is a time to worry about that. You knew full well what you were doing and now you fear that poor girl finding out about your sordid treachery? Isn't that something you should have broached much earlier?" Everilda taunted him.

She had her eyes affixed on the weak shadow of a man who couldn't even have the gusto to be seen near the place where some unlikely eyes might be wandering over his "precious" Isra. Or not so, since he was doing the dirty on both of them.

Yes, it is the same Jonathan. Oh my. The very same who had been doing his utmost to get to immortality with Isra. In the romantic sense, anyway. But now who is this striking fair-haired lady? Astrid wondered.

He was feeling uneasy regarding this new onlooker and how she fitted into the Jonathan/Isra entanglement.

"But I would have met with you anywhere Everi, except here," Jonathan expressed in a callous tone.

The fear seemed to escape his lips with every breath, but yet it remained within him as he appeared to be clutching his stomach, evidently anxious of them being right out here, the only location where Isra could suddenly materialize at a moment's notice much to his horror.

"Yes, well I chose here for a reason!" Everilda practically screeched at him back.

Her blue eyes were almost red with rage, apparently bleeding as she scowled and cursed at Jonathan without a care. Of course, they were just without the physical entity of blood. But still, since Everilda was a witch and Jonathan was—well, a mortal—Astrid figured that blood could still be spilled because this was one hell of an angry lady, one he had barely even begun to fathom, but so far, he had worked out she was the other woman in this conundrum of sorts that Jonathan had been conducting between himself, Isra, and now this not so fine lady.

"Ah! You deceitful, conceited witch! You did this deliberately!" Jonathan exclaimed in response.

He was furious that Everilda had gone so far as to arrange a meeting right outside Wingdom's of all dwellings. And how convenient that it was set up to be the residence right where Isra could easily get wind of their vile affair!

"Yes, well Isra has to find out soon enough! I've just sped up the proceedings!" Everilda huffed.

Aha. So this lady actually knew Isra, not just knew of, but knew personally. *Now isn't that an interesting puzzle piece to this mysterious enigma?* Astrid posed in thought as he stood back in the shadows soaking all this in.

"You are disgraceful! You venomous, wicked old hag!" Jonathan yelled at her back.

He was so loud that he scared off a brown and beige tawny owl that had taken solace in the nearby cherry tree. God knows what that creature had been thinking listening to these two bawling and yammering at each other.

Ha, disgraceful? She's shown you up for the pathetic piece of shit you are and you call her disgraceful? I mean, pardon me, but did you not just admit you were dangling two women by your hind quarters? Toying with them. And having your merry way? Correct me if I am wrong. But it is you that is disgraceful, lad, Astrid cajoled to himself in thought regarding the treacherous Jonathan. His train of thought sounded menacing now.

The raven was clearly very angry with Jonathan for how he had been operating himself in regards to Isra, something that would lead one to believe that dear old Astrid had some fondness for Isra. Not that the endearing raven would ever confess to it. But anyway, that could hold space in time, for Astrid was out here witnessing the grand confrontation between Jonathan and Everilda. And so there were many more matters to be dealt with at the time than some feelings.

Everilda stood in front of Jonathan looking like the cat that got the cream, almost licking her lips as she sneered at him without uttering a word. Jonathan was not pleased, having been dragged out here after midnight only to find himself tricked into meeting Everilda right by the place he did not want to be. Coincidence? One would say not.

But hey, you could almost feel sorry for the poor simpering fool. Jonathan had been well and truly taken in by Everilda's alluring emotional manner for she had gotten a message to him magically. This message was deeply profound but filled with emotional blackmail that had not only convinced him that she needed him—ha, what a joke that was!—but Everilda had also succeeded in manipulating Jonathan by telling him she had needed to see him urgently.

Of course, you don't need me to tell you that the poor boy had fallen for it without hesitation, hurling himself out of his bed to come here unannounced. What an idiot. But then Everilda had always proclaimed that Jonathan was bloody stupid even when she was liaising with his brother, Valien. Even then she'd tapped into Jonathan's lack of direction and common sense in the manner where he'd take action without giving it any thought.

"Yes, well. Needs must," Everilda commented. She sounded thoroughly pleased with herself for getting the better of this man who had clearly thought he would be able to make a fool of her.

Oh no, honey. I'm not as dumb as you perceive me to be! I'm sure you'd rather I'd be as dense as Isra has been, but oh no, I'm smarter than her, Everilda countered to herself regarding Jonathan in a subliminal train of thought.

"Needs must, dear? Funny how one comments on need when she sends her mystical messenger to me, shuffling around in the dense bracken almost scaring me witless as it tells me your enlightening revelation," Jonathan chided with spit emitting from his mouth.

He was evidently very angry with Everilda, although that might be due to the fact she had drawn him up like a horse and carriage, laying him into play right where she wanted him but forgetting to tell him that he was going to be on the backseat.

"Oh, that was the naughtiest trick, dear Everi, wasn't it?" Jonathan probed. Apparently, he was not satisfied with brawling with her in the grounds of Wingdom's Academy for the last few minutes.

"Yes, well..." was all that Everilda could muster as a reply.

The fair-haired witch suddenly became silent, not saying anything further. Everilda turned her head away from Jonathan, showing him her back. How peculiar, but why was she doing this?

Jonathan was mirroring Everilda, having watched her go quiet at once. Puzzled, he tried to work out why, but the answer was right among them, staring across their bewildered faces as they stood watching the entire scene.

"Oh, wait a second," Astrid gasped. "No, it can't be..." he exclaimed in shock.

13

No sooner had he said those words than his worst realization was confirmed. It was her. Clear as day. Isra stood by the gray stone steps of Wingdom's.

Astrid recognized her instantly even though she was barely dressed in a thin lacy white nightgown, revealing just a tiny bit of leg above her ankles. Her eyes were harsh and cold and the green shimmer seemed to light up the way that led to Jonathan and Everilda. Isra met Everilda's silence with a melancholy gaze before taking her eyes away as she crossed her arms in an angry stance, turning to Jonathan with an icy stare.

"Oh, this can't be good," Astrid muttered.

But before the raven could do or say anything, Isra began striding over to the unrighteous twosome, Jonathan and Everilda.

"Well, I never planned to see both of you in my midst at the same dwelling! I had hoped there would be some mistake!" she said quietly as if anticipating at least one of them to correct her.

Alas, that was not to be as Everilda turned to face Isra with a furrowed brow, only to confirm Isra's greatest fear.

"I am afraid it is all true. You and I share a common denominator.

Not only are we friends, dear girl, but we share the same pathetic coward of a man."

~

ISRA SAID NOTHING, only mirroring the existential silence that surrounded the three troubled souls in the wee hours of whom had just learned they were connected in ways they had not known. Well, Isra had learned they were, anyhow. Jonathan and Everilda had been carrying on with this charade right under Isra's nose for many moons, both having been fully aware of Isra's involvement in their interesting triangle of sorts.

Astrid could only sit by and examine the situation with a rigorous eye. He had expected Isra to scream and yell at them both by now, or cast out an array of unsought insults but no, she had not succumbed to any of that. Instead, the young witch maintained a calm demeanor which only made Jonathan tremble in his boots. The perilous worm he was!

"Surely she's angry, but no? Oh my, this is worse than I had thought," Astrid chattered away to himself, taking extreme caution in ensuring he was not heard, for not only was he in the presence of a mortal but two witches, one of which he was sure would be unleashing hell on earth at any given moment.

Or at least I expected she would be! She is way too calm for a girl who has just found out her best friend has been carrying on with her handsome yet egoistical snake of a man behind her back, Astrid mused to himself sullenly in thought. *If only there was something I could do or even say. But what would I say? She doesn't even know me. For all she knows I could be a foe. It's clear to me that she does not trust anyone and even more so now. How could I even begin the conversation? She has no reason to accept my comfort or my friendship.*

Astrid continued mulling over to himself round and round again as he considered all the options in reaching out to Isra, although such an act would be considered strictly forbidden as far as the "on high" was concerned. Samuel was the only one who was allowed to get involved personally in the matters of these dark-hearted souls.

"I am damned if I do and damned if I don't. Why did I have to get myself into this situation? I am very much fond of this lost girl, and I fear now she will disappear into isolation. And who can blame her for doing so?" he asked himself in a meek tone. "Perhaps it is best I do not fly away just yet. She may need me. I should keep watch on the proceedings, just to lay a friendly eye on her if nothing else." Astrid said to himself although out loud as if he were agreeing with a strong yet firm confidante.

Meanwhile Isra's unrelenting, hard as nails resolve was not wavering. Not by an inch. She prevailed in only glaring at both Everilda and Jonathan. Neither of them had the audacity to give her eye contact which could be seen as a good or bad thing, depending on how you looked at it. Don't forget this was a witch who had just witnessed her best friend and man betraying her in a most apathetic way. After what seemed like an eternity of silence, the hardened witch finally spoke, addressing her foes in kind.

"A pathetic man, eh? Well, I must say Evie, I never expected his victim to be you. I have to regain my composure, for this was something I was not prepared for. However..."

Isra paused, narrowing her eyes at Everilda with an even icier stare, barely even acknowledging the girl she thought of as her closest and most endearing friend.

"It does explain the interrogations you pursued ceaselessly. Especially ... the 'things that are not meant for you' evasive mannerism, but hey, I understand your meaning now, don't I?" Isra countered in a sarcastic manner.

The comment was clearly aimed at Everilda's vagueness that she had displayed in that calm yet viscous demeanor she demonstrated back when they shared that awkward coffee in Everilda's dwelling.

"Yes. I am sorry," Everilda mouthed with no empathy at all. It was apparent to all and sundry that she wasn't sorry at all.

"I am not really one that is interested in the details after such an injustice has occurred. I will commune with you later," Isra addressed Everilda plainly.

Isra regarded her so-called friend with such cold-hearted venom that the fair-haired witch had no comprehension of where she stood with Isra. And more importantly, whether there would be some kind of fiery backlash about to come Everilda's way.

"As for you," Isra pointed at Jonathan, "how novel of you to enchant two ladies in your midst and not know they were wonderfully acquainted, both holding you highly in their sights."

Isra conducted this speech in such a calm and controlled deportment that she did seem friendly in her tone, but again Jonathan had no clue on whether she was maddened enough to hack off his manly parts with one strike. Not that he didn't deserve that because by golly, he did.

So is she going to castrate me? Or am I in for a harrowing lecture instead of something terribly grotesque? Jonathan chortled in thought. He was almost mumbling to himself as he hovered between quivering with fear and resounding no emotion at all.

"Yes," Jonathan piped up with eagerness. Maybe a little too much as he addressed Isra. "I have done the most terrible thing. I deserve to be punished."

"Yes, and punished you shall be."

Isra motioned with a fluttering hand before walking away. She ventured over the gray steps, not caring what Jonathan said or did because now was not a time to be concerned over anyone. Jonathan, however, took the hint and disappeared before anyone could notice his exit. His lingering shadow dissipated as he ran through the mass of trees, heading back to his home domain. The only thought that was present in the mortal's mind revolved around one person, and it was no surprise who it was.

But hang on, where did Everilda get to? Oh, it's no matter, as long as she is not near me.

Cowardice as ever, all Jonathan was worried about was the backlash that would surely be heading his way at any time. "At least I managed to escape without anyone noticing my departure," he mumbled reassuringly to himself.

∾

ONLY MUCH TO Jonathan's disappointment, someone had seen him leave the chaos behind in his wake. Astrid the raven was still present, hiding around the corner of the stone-gray steps. He was now in an arm's reach from Isra of whom he had observed was sitting down on the steps appearing to have her head down, just like she had done in his vision of her.

Oh my, it is true then, Astrid realized in his thoughts. *I can't believe it. Everything the "on high" said was absolutely spot on. They didn't miss a single trick. They saw this long before she was going to transpire into this very state she is now in which she is turning away from everything she ever knew. And who would even begin to be able to fathom that she would turn so cold when she discovered the betrayal that laid her in the midst? Of course, it had to be "on high."*

Astrid mused quietly inside his mind, mulling over everything. *Do you know something else? Samuel was also correct down to the finest detail. Why did I never see it? I didn't even comprehend the fact that she was headed for darkness, but now I see it. Oh, by hell, do I see it. Darn it. I miss things too easily, allowing myself to get caught up in the fickle feelings I have for her. Damn me.* Astrid cussed sullenly in thought to himself.

Still on the premise of keeping an eye on Isra, Astrid crept around the corner watching the overwrought Isra who was still situated on the grand gray steps with her long, flowing, lace nightgown billowing out in the wind.

It was still the small wee hours and would be a good few hours before dawn. The harsh navy-blue sky barely showed any light, but that which shone from the glowing moon as its warmth descended down from the darkened skies made it seem a little more overcast tonight than usual for some reason. A symbol, perhaps, of the energy that was about to envelope the land, or so it had been foretold.

As for Isra, she looked tired as she sat there most desolate. Her face was paler than usual in color. She appeared to be withdrawn as if she was there but not really present at the moment. Her emerald green eyes barely even acknowledged the fact that it was once again pelting down with rain. The rain drops soaked Isra's slim body to the skin, making her nightdress cling to her, only bringing more prominence to her entrancing shape. Isra was almost resounding that same guise a grieving widow would display when she was in denial of her loss.

Really, Astrid thought that Isra ought to be in her chamber sleeping in silky satin sheets, but the raven made a mental note to himself that it wasn't likely Isra would be entertaining any form of rest for the foreseeable future. This was the absolute pitfall for Isra. First, she'd had the angry moment where she had a verbal standoff with both Everilda and Jonathan, but now both of them had absconded away. Isra was alone. She had no need to keep wearing her tough facade.

Astrid wondered if it would be too forward to sit with her for a while, to comfort her in her hour of need. One might find it a little presumptuous of him and he'd surely be scolded if Samuel got wind of it. But Astrid did not care.

As far as he was concerned, this was personal for him now. He felt a duty to be here for her. This witch that had just had the floor whipped from under her feet, left out in the cold, and was now wavering on the brink of self-destruction. But still, Isra didn't look like she was about to do something that would be wholly terrible. She appeared to be emotionally numb. Perhaps withdrawn. As she was isolated in this wilderness in the middle of the night. But still, there's always hope, right?

That was what Astrid was banking on. Damn, he'd put his very soul on the line for it if he could. But being a raven, he'd doubt that kind of bargain would be ever accepted from the ones in charge, those that were the "on high." Let's face it; Astrid wasn't even supposed to be involved in Isra's life at this very delicate stage she was at. If anyone ever got wind of this, Astrid could rest assured that Samuel would throw the most vile hissy fit known to man. It is also safe to say that the light bringers would be majorly pissed at him.

Yes, let's not draw extra attention to ourselves when we don't need that kind of exposure just yet. Astrid murmured to himself in thought.

Astrid decided that he'd spent enough time hiding himself away. He was going to be bold for once in making himself known. Yes, this could come across as a rather brash and unplanned decision but Astrid was yearning to be close with Isra. After all, he'd kept so much distance between them for a while now. He would have to make himself visible in her sight sooner or later. And what better time than now? It was a moment where Isra really needed someone.

Even if it was only for a fleeting minute where they both sat silent in the rain, perhaps he could do some good by being by the witch's side. When Astrid considered the matter frugally he presumed that no harm would commence if he was to momentarily brush up beside Isra, looking into her glowing emerald green eyes just for a second.

"Fuck it," Astrid cajoled to himself in an annoyed tone.

Why am I even discussing this with myself? I know she's in need of my assistance. I know she doesn't resemble a threat to me. Neither will she demonstrate any harm toward my person. I am just going to sidle on over to her and be done with it. Enough procrastination. I'm going in there. I'll perch myself up right before her very eyes and we will see what emerges. And now I sound like a crazed maniac going over this like a spinning wheel in my head. Goodness, Astrid, get a blooming grip, will you? The raven cursed himself with his thoughtful words once again.

So gently coming from around the corner of the gray stone steps, Astrid breathed in a little as he came toward Isra, stopping for a second as he found himself at her feet. It was amazing really. He was right before her, but she hadn't even noticed him. Isra still had her head down and it appeared as if the maiden was indeed weeping.

Oh no, what a sight. I did not want to witness this. Astrid hesitated with a low gaze.

But still, there was something intriguing about her. It was almost like a wave of energy hit Astrid from all directions as he found himself enchanted by Isra's presence even with her being engulfed in so much sorrow. As the tears streamed down her perfectly serene face it was clear for Astrid to see that there was so much more inside this young soul than he had anticipated. A captivating yet alluring energy surrounded her. It was one of mysticism.

There was that wistful look about her that charmed any unsuspecting friend or foe that dared to enter the very fragments of her damaged soul that said, "Come in and open me up," and Astrid had to admit that he too was tempted to discover more about Isra. The whys and wherefores of who she was. He wanted to learn why she was like this. What could have happened in her life to shape her up to be this way? He was dead curious at how someone so young had such a stiff and formal attitude around emotions ... Well, basically any kind of feeling.

The raven was still by Isra's feet when suddenly the witch looked down upon him.

"Oh my," Astrid whispered calmly.

He was almost considering the notion as to whether he should fly off now before something could go horribly wrong. It was apparent that Astrid was so deeply worried about upsetting Isra, for if just one sound of his claws scratching against the gray stone steps startled her he would be deeply grieved by it.

Astrid was not one for conflict. And he certainly didn't want to be somebody that instigated it either. But how amazed Astrid was when Isra extended her arm downward to him. She was no longer weeping as she left her arm positioned just above the ground in midair awaiting him to step onto it. It was bewildering, but here she was, allowing something truly magical to commence.

He found it to be an inviting yet surprising gesture on her part, one that had sent Astrid a little delirious as he had expected her to run off or shoo him away.

"Oh my, giddiness!" Astrid exclaimed in disbelief, ambling over to climb onto Isra's arm before settling down, realizing he was being observed by Isra's bold yet mysterious emerald green eyes, an inquisitive look one might say but one that only beguiled and enchanted him.

Astrid was shocked at just how much of a close proximity he had been allowed to have with her. It might have sounded nonsensical, but the raven felt very blessed and privileged to have such an encounter with the very one he had been yearning for.

However, Isra had seen Astrid's nervous disposition as he quietly and yet quickly made it over to her arm. She said nothing to him, only smiling at him in a fond and yet endearing manner. If Astrid were a human, he'd have been flashing beetroot red cheeks of shyness right about now. Black feathers had something going for them, that was for sure.

"Do not fear me, friend. For I have no intent to place any kind of harm on you," Isra whispered in a soft voice.

There was something really calm in the manner of how she spoke, clearly not the same displeasing venom she had verbally demonstrated earlier. It was sweet as if her throat had been dipped in honey. Isra's eyes met Astrid's in a somewhat awkward yet mesmerizing stare. At least it was all butterfingers for Astrid as he was rather awestruck at her kindness and how gentle she was in allowing him to rest on the crook of her arm.

Astrid couldn't utter a single syllable and instead the raven was forced to sit back and collect his thoughts as he was overwhelmed by this encouraging experience. Never in his life did he imagine he'd get to meet Isra in this way or even at all, so it was remarkable to say the least.

"I should get back to Samuel," he murmured to himself as he considered what Isra would do next.

This had been a wonderful opportunity, one he had not seen coming to fruition. Astrid felt so blessed to be able to have this close up encounter but now the sadness was coming upon him as he realized he'd have to leave things back to the "on high" and in Samuel's domain.

I suppose I could pop back here and there, just to keep a close eye on her, Astrid pondered quietly as Isra's bright green eyes were still all over his being.

Still, some things can only last for so long. Astrid knew that.

Eventually this transfixing moment where two minds met as one would have to come to an inevitable close if only for a short period of time because Astrid was not going anywhere. No, he'd risk Samuel's wrath and fury in order to stay at arm's length where this young darkened soul was concerned. He'd sacrifice it all just to be in her grasp. At least to clap his eyes on her mesmerizing form just to see how she was getting along.

Yes, well needs must, Astrid muttered to himself in thought. *I must depart now before Samuel sends out a search party and I certainly do not want him to become even more cross with me.*

Astrid looked up at Isra with a cheery half smile as if he was acknowledging some part of himself that wasn't quite able to break away from her sight. But he had to do it.

"It's all for the greater glory," he whispered quietly to himself, glancing up at the night that was softly disintegrating into dawn as gentle yellow hues began to peek out amongst the trees surrounding Wingdom's Academy.

So before anything else could deter him from leaving, Astrid spread out his wings and wasted no time in soaring into the moonlit skies.

14

Isra sat up straight in her chair, her head turned toward the window as Magnus Wingdom drawled on about transfiguration or transformation. Isra wasn't too sure as she hadn't been paying attention, and instead daydreaming with her glowing green eyes focused on the cherry tree outside.

Oh, how she longed to get out of this debauchery and sit beside that tree. To feel its warmth as she nestled up against its rough bark and minded her own business just sitting outside, isolating herself away from everyone and everything. Isra especially wanted to segregate herself off from Everilda of whom was only three seats away from her, positioned at the front of their classroom. Not that it was much of a class you understand, merely just Magnus Wingdom rabbiting on about this, that, and the other.

And what use do I have for transformation anyway? Isra asked herself as she found her mind reentering the room. Her focus seemed to land haphazardly on Everilda who glared at every person who happened to meet the range of her eyesight.

Wow, she's moody for someone who just reigned absolute chaos on her companion's life, but it is no matter. Really, I will soldier on despite it all, Isra continued in her thoughts as she slipped back into what appeared to be a daydream, finding herself straying away from the room and losing focus as she drifted into another stratosphere.

$$\sim$$

"Well, I must say this is a pleasant meeting," Everilda chided from the corner of the room. Her sapphire eyes glinted at Isra from where she stood in the darkness.

"Evie! I didn't expect to find anyone else around," Isra gasped in shock at finding Everilda here.

"Neither did I," was all Everilda could muster as a reply.

Isra suddenly turned her attention to the scene around her. The harsh stone walls in blackened murky shades of dull browns now appeared white as a yellow light shone out in the distance.

It couldn't be, could it? No, not that. It cannot be, Isra thought to herself. This is just a layman's world after all. One cannot expect such a thing after so much turmoil, but yet I see it. Oh, how bright and enchanting it is.

She turned to Everilda once more, addressing her friend in a formal tone. "I must go now, for the light is calling my name. I am curious to see where it leads me," Isra recited in a wistful voice as if dreams were colliding down her throat and lingering in the midst of imagination and wonder.

"Oh, go if you must!" Everilda retorted with a cruel laugh before pausing as her smile became that one would wear when they had enacted something truly sinister in nature. "But remember, life is just one big illusion!" She shouted out after Isra.

However, Isra did not hear Everilda's comment for she was wandering down the long and narrow path. It was so dark that only the tiny yellow lights from the candle flames gave any indication of where it might lead. It seemed to go on forever as Isra kept on walking on the cold stone floor, finding herself in more unfamiliar terrain as the path kept on dwindling further down.

"I wonder if there is an end to this. I just want to see where it leads me. Is that honestly so wrong?" Isra asked herself with a meek curiosity. There was a deep yearning within her to reach the finish line of this and discover whatever may be waiting when she found it.

Finally, after what seemed an eternity, an opening was revealed at the end of the long unwinding path, making it appear like a tunnel as it grew more and more narrow and Isra got closer to the thing that was the source of all the golden yellow light.

Oh, she couldn't believe what she was looking at. There Jonathan stood right in front of her dressed entirely in black. A black top hat, the same as when she had first laid eyes on him adorned his head and the rest of his clothing was the same apart from delicate white silk breeches that went almost down to his ankles and shielded his manly parts. Whereas on his feet, he had on shiny black leather shoes matching the rest of him. How morbid he looked and yet there was something rather symbolic about the way he stood in front of her. A remorseful glance came from him as he pulled out a small trinket box from his pocket, extending it to Isra in a sort of warm gesture.

What on earth could this be? she thought. *No way can it be that? No way in hell on earth is it what I deem it to be. But stranger things have happened.*

Not even hesitating for a second, Isra accepted the box from Jonathan with the sheer desire to pry it open right here at this moment. The pressure of it was overwhelming as she held the box in her cold hands. How anxious she was as she lifted up the lid of the elegant trinket box to reveal a solid gold ring with a square-cut diamond in the center staring back at her. She almost dropped the box in amazement.

"Oh gosh," Isra whispered, almost crying as she stared at the ring in horrific disbelief.

Jonathan began to weep now, expressing his emotional disdain as he cried out, "I am sorry, but this is what I cannot give you. Everilda has me bound to her will and until you break her spell, I am forever cursed to be hers."

Isra took a second to process this revelation, allowing it to sink in as it revolved her mind, replaying over and over again with the words, "I am forever cursed to be hers. I am forever cursed to be hers."

Isra could not forget those obstinate and fearful words that Jonathan had uttered as he wept bitterly. His eyes showed nothing but loss and regret of what his life could have been, but now Isra could see that was never ever going to be. Jonathan could never have been hers. She could never have attained him successfully even if she had used magic.

Everilda had seen to that. It was now becoming so clear what was really occurring in the wake of her premise. Seeing Jonathan in this painful and fragmented state showed her a different side of the mortal man, one she had never recalled seeing from him. He'd evidently hidden it from her the whole time she had been by his side, not that it was a very long courting period they'd had, you understand, but still it made perfect sense.

Isra took her focus away from her train of recurring thoughts and looked back at Jonathan for what she knew would be the very last time. And as it happened, the mortal only had one thing to say to her, gazing at her once again, looking her in the eyes as he uttered gravely.

"She will not release me. Please believe me," Jonathan proclaimed in a heartfelt tone while mustering all his strength. "She will never let me go."

It was a tone that spoke of a harsh and cruel fate he had been subjected to all because of the vengeful witch he had aligned himself with all those years ago. If only he had turned away when he'd had the chance, but the mortal man had not had good judgment and so succumbed to his lust. It was unfortunate that the ultimate price to pay was to lose his only chance at real love; however, this was how the world worked. It was deemed that the one thing you desire the most was to be stolen from you callously when you allowed yourself to be taken over by those that reared their ugly heads in irrefutable obscurity.

It was simply how things were taken care of and how karma always won out in the end. A bittersweet notion some would say, but maybe it was also poetic justice for Jonathan to lose that tiny shred of good fortune the kind and deserving world might have bestowed upon him because he had been so shallow and greedy.

Isra had totally lost all sense of feeling as she stared into Jonathan's cold, dark brown eyes before they began to blur away from her as did the scene around her. Before Isra could even question what on earth was transpiring between her and Jonathan, the dark world she had known for those brief moments had totally vanished as she found herself back in the room, staring at Magnus Wingdom.

Oh, good gracious, Isra thought. *That was a daydream? It felt so real. But wait...*

She questioned the notion of that for a moment. *Suppose it wasn't as much of a daydream as I presume it to be? I mean, let's say that Jonathan has been cursed by Everilda and that was the only way of him letting me know. It is possible, one could guess. I know there is something inside me that can tap into that which is unknown but this felt so surreal. It was almost like a visionary tale being played out in my mind, but how can that be? I was sitting here bored out of my skull for one fragment of a second and the next I was in that tunnel. How could one acccomplish such feats in a dull classroom?*

"I must learn more about these abilities I possess," Isra whispered to herself although apparently, she wasn't as quiet as she had hoped she would be.

Magnus Wingdom swiftly struck his golden staff embedded with a large rounded jet-black onyx in the center violently against the enormous blackboard while staring directly at Isra. The sound of it was so loud it shook the room, causing everyone to lay their eyes on Isra.

"Do you have something relevant the class should indeed hear, Miss Isra?" he called out in a brash tone.

"No, sir," Isra excused herself. "I was merely just thinking out a complicated conundrum to myself. I didn't mean to share so vocally."

"Ahem, yes. Well, that may be," he chided her sternly. "But please do remember you are here to learn the art of transfiguration, not dawdling on in your fantasy bubble, wherever it is."

"Yes, Magnus," Isra answered him politely although there was a pause. Suddenly it dawned on her that this classroom, this place of study and learning was not meant for her any longer. She needed to get herself out of here before too long as something else was beckoning her.

"May I be excused for a moment, sir?" Isra requested. She was banking on the idea that he would allow her to take her leave despite the horrid mood he was in.

Magnus Wingdom huffed as if he found something really irritating about Isra wanting to swan off and be elsewhere. After all, she had virtually no respect for his teachings whatsoever and most of the time yawned her way through his tedious lessons, if they could even be classed as such. Because honestly Isra was the type that would sit yearning for something a bit more adventurous. Something that captivated the inner rebel that desired to break free from her body and discover all the wondrously forbidden array of goodies that life had to offer.

"Well, if you must!" he came back at her gruffly, still obviously very annoyed at her lack of respect for him.

"Thank you, sir," Isra announced in a false sweet tone.

She didn't need any further prodding. Time was of the essence especially when you wanted to get something done real fast before anyone else could decipher just what you were up to.

Isra haphazardly stood up in a flurry from her chair before she carelessly tossed it under the slightly orange tinged oak desk. It was apparent to all in succession that she was in a hurry. And it came as no surprise that she dashed across the room, rushing feet first to the solid, dark brown wooden door before anyone could stop her. Only there was something else intriguing about this puzzle because Isra was not the only student making haste in having a quick getaway. Before her very eyes as Isra stood by the door, she suddenly noticed that Everilda had also stood up from her seat. She was now rising up to address the rest of the room.

No way can this be real! Isra mused sarcastically in thought, almost amused at the situation playing out right before her.

But yes, it was indeed true. Everilda had swiftly stood up from her chair and was now facing Magnus Wingdom. The fair-haired girl looked him dead in those murky blue eyes. And what a brave soul she was for even gearing up to defy such a coven master in the presence of all her peers.

Damn, I would not want to be in her shoes. Oh no, not in a million lifetimes, Isra scoffed in quiet hilarity to herself.

For she had been allowed absence by Magnus, but Everilda on the other hand? Hmmm, perhaps not so as he was still eyeballing her like she was something standing out amongst the crowd that he really wanted to take a shot at. He was so gloriously angry at her stance for getting up so unceremoniously from her seat.

Oh golly, she'd be in for it if she didn't have a good reason for wanting to escape. But why does she want to slip away now that I am? Isra pondered in thought. *Is she honestly that desperate to get a rise from me? To copy my stance in some grand gesture making herself look as though we are on the same side because honestly the mere idea of it is preposterous! Is this some kind of game in which I am the queen and she takes on the role of the poor crushed knight in order to win my affections? All I can see is desperation coming off her in waves. It really is pathetic but then she is that type of human. Always seeking some kind of approval from others, sad really. But not to worry for one must not dwell on these matters. Let's see how our tenacious professor takes her little escapade to oblivion.*

Everilda made her plea, standing before the faculty member of Wingdom's as she began to speak in a low yet also very charming voice. How ironic, considering she wanted to be flavor of the month with him all of a sudden.

Yes, very convenient my dear, I must say, Isra mocked sullenly to herself completely interrupting Everilda's little speech evidently before she could even begin as the fair-haired witch stopped before she had even opened her mouth. Isra could only respond with a snigger. Oh, how amusing indeed! *But come on; let's see what tedious excuse you have concocted up for yourself,* Isra mused quietly.

"If you please, sir," Everilda started to emit her verbal plea, but Magnus who was already glaring at the rapturous witch was having none of it.

"If I please? My dear, before you even command such a sentence, you've already voiced such discontent for my lessons. And let me guess, you disregard them as unnecessary and probably rather dull for your impeccable tastes, am I right?" he finished, snapping at her with his reprimand.

He couldn't have put it any more bluntly if he had tried. Honestly it was a brutal deliverance of truth from the presumed pompous and stuffy leader. Isra had to admit she was slightly impressed with him even though she had always found him to be rather dull. Everilda however continued to press on, not discouraged at all by Magnus Wingdom's verbally blasting her.

"Yes, but Isra gets to abscond, does she not?" Everilda challenged him with a brash smile that also portrayed her resentment and sheer bitterness. The way it came off her tongue sounded so sour could only further confirm that she was mighty angry that Isra was getting special privileges. That was how she was viewing it, anyhow.

Magnus was heated in his reply to Everilda stating it in a profound manner, "Yes, but many of my students choose to leave my classes for whatever reason they deem fit. And I will not comment on it any further."

"Wow," was all that Everilda could muster, clearly appalled by Magnus's attitude toward her.

He was making it seem like Isra was the teacher's pet all of a sudden, but Everilda was not impressed by his change in opinions because she knew that Isra was as much of a delinquent as she. If not even worse. But Everilda began to smell something else about this special case and that was why she suspected that Isra was in receipt of special treatment.

Isra was still standing by the door frame as an onlooker that was witness to the entire debacle between Everilda and Magnus. It made her feel quite awkward as she still wasn't entirely sure of Everilda's intent. Isra wasn't sure as to why Everilda was so dead set on also leaving the lesson, but wonders would never cease when it came to Everilda.

Isra decided to speak up, having had enough of being present to such a pitiful squabble between Everilda and Magnus. She took a deep breath before lowering her tone a little in order to maintain a bit of respect for her elder; as unorthodox as it sounded as she didn't find Magnus at all endearing. But she had decided upon this sweetened strategy just to remove herself from this disastrous plight.

"If you please, sir," Isra began, hilariously in the same way as Everilda had started her bargaining, but Isra had far more meticulous ways to garner favor than her foe, for she was going to take a more methodical approach to have things go her way.

"I should be taking my leave now but, I don't wish to impose on anyone. I would respectfully request that I am formally excused and hope no malice has been incurred today as a result of my departure," Isra uttered in a bold yet kind feeling voice. She couldn't have been more diplomatic if she had tried.

And what's more, it was clearly winning over old Magnus because for the first time ever, Isra actually caught a smile bearing across the old man's face.

"Yes, dear. All graciously understood. You may go," he answered, quickly returning his attention to Everilda.

Isra couldn't help but turn toward her foe as she stood by the edge of the doorway flashing a smug grin in Everilda's direction much to the fair-haired witch's annoyance. Everilda had a face like thunder.

Not so cocky now are we, my dear? Isra mused in sardonic thought as she made her exit leaving Everilda left alone with the very hot-tempered professor.

Whatever it was that was going to occur between her fiery foe and the head of Wingdom's Academy, Isra certainly did not need to have the knowledge of it. She had matters of her own interest to attend to.

15

____

Back in Spirisity, business was undoubtedly on the agenda. Samuel sat back in his red velvet armchair looking up at the ceiling in a perplexed manner. Although Samuel didn't look to be especially comfortable, he did have his back pressed against the soft material and appeared to be preoccupied with a particular problem. That enigmatic mind of his seemed to be elsewhere as he glared at the clock in an irritated fashion.

"I told that raven to be on time. Why is he late?" Samuel asked himself as he awaited the moment his plush royal blue curtain would burst open to announce the arrival of Astrid. "Always off gallivanting. Never on time when I summon him to be in my midst."

Samuel commented in a flustered tone, presuming that Astrid was out somewhere feasting to his heart's content on some delicious, juicy worms. He twitched his head forward glowering upon the blue curtain as his silver rimmed, moon-shaped spectacles focused on the shape of it, expecting it to swing forth at any moment.

Come on. It's got to be any moment now. We have matters of importance to discuss here concerning the witch, Samuel mused with impatience to himself in thought, plainly annoyed at Astrid's lack of punctuality.

Samuel did take his eyes away from the curtain for feeling he might miss something. He had that hooked look about him whereby he stared deeply into the plush midnight blue material, almost becoming one with it he was so focused on his subject. As if on command, the plucky raven charged through the curtain as he made his entrance. Undeniably Astrid was a little distracted as he acknowledged the fact that he was impeccably late.

"Ah, yes. My apologies, Samuel," Astrid chortled as he caught his breath after having such a long, stressful flight to get here. "It has been a most enthralling day," he added in, noticing Samuel's displeasure as the light bringer carefully brought his moon rimmed glasses back to rest upon his nose.

Astrid edged forward, perching himself on Samuel's desk in anticipation of whatever his master had summoned him for.

"I can see that you've had a thrilling time, Astrid," Samuel refuted the raven in a melancholic voice. "I have been graciously awaiting your arrival. I have something of great importance to discuss with you."

Samuel turned to the left of him, just beyond his antique mahogany desk, revealing an onlooker who had evidently sat there for the entire duration of this conversation.

Although appearing very much human in his peachy coloring that adorned the young man's form, the onlooker adjacent to Samuel's left seemed to have a beguiling yet mystical way about him as he gave Astrid the raven a cautionary stare. Perhaps this new player of whom was named James was also very much displeased over the raven's lateness. But it wasn't overly transparent as the man whose name was James said absolutely nothing to Astrid in return.

It was peculiar to say the least, but Astrid felt very uncomfortable as James continued to cross-examine him with a sharp glance. There was notably a rivalry of sorts between the two males as Astrid proceeded to respond to James with a dead-center stare. The raven made haste in taking note of James's light brown eyes almost glinting like the sun in Samuel's darkened quarters. It was paradoxical as the place rarely saw daylight since it was in the business of fighting adversaries who had switched over to the dark.

Astrid also observed that James had mousy brown hair coming down to his neck. Only unlike Samuel's it was not slicked back, it was more straight in a tidier fashion leaving him with a bare neck only further confirming to Astrid that James was indeed a human.

What in the heavens? Astrid cursed in thought, still maintaining eye contact with James in unison. *Who the hell is this guy and why is he staring at me?* Astrid almost sounded out in thought, being careful to glance over at Samuel, who of course could read minds better than most. Just one look from the stern light bringer would have brought Astrid's reverie to a devastating end.

Astrid was not certain on why he was being glared at in this manner, but James was very much focused on Astrid, not giving the raven an inch of leeway as he refused to look away. It was ironic when you consider that both parties had never met, but before Astrid could mull over this any further, he was halted in his tracks as Samuel displayed a blazing look in the raven's direction. However, Samuel didn't waste any time in disclosing why they were all here in his humble abode.

"Ah, yes. This is James from the 'on high' and he is here to assist us with our complex calamity regarding the feisty young enchantress you will soon come to know as Lady Isra of the dark," Samuel said, turning his head toward James in a welcoming manner. "But first, we must talk about the small matter of you sneaking into Wingdom's Academy in the dead of night!" Samuel added, sounding menacing as he waved an offensive finger at Astrid as if to scold him for his misdeed.

Oh shit! Astrid thought immediately. *I have been caught black feathered and I bet this pesky James character had his eyeballs all over me that night! Sneaky little human he is! I bet he sleeps with his sword right underneath him,* Astrid countered to himself sarcastically, imagining James being one of those types that the "on high" rewarded for that stealthy kind of behavior. *Those annoying cretins from "on high" with their rules and regulations. Telling you that you must not do this and don't do that.* The raven cussed to himself, obviously very irritated by this new development.

Samuel was clearly becoming inpatient at Astrid's insolence of not answering him, so he took his interrogation further. "Oh, thought you'd go unnoticed, did you? Barging your way into the very same dwelling that our witch calls home. Charging in there like a fathomless knight in the small wee hours? You honestly thought nobody would see you? My goodness, Astrid, just where is your head?" Samuel probed.

Astrid raised his eyebrows in defense as he looked at Samuel boldly. "Yes, well, while my actions have been considered impure, please understand that I have been in the thick of it. I've seen the very event that is going to make her turn the tide. I have witnessed the heartbreak that has made her seek the shadows. I only went in that vagrant place to seek shelter from the storm that was brewing above," Astrid explained, noting Samuel's reaction to his cautionary tale.

It seemed that Samuel had an understanding of Astrid's reasons and why he'd ventured into Wingdom's Academy in the small hours despite Astrid's very prominent affections for Isra, the subject in question that had forced this meeting between himself, Astrid, and James.

"All right, Astrid," Samuel acknowledged. "I can see your intent was not one of malice, but please remember your place in the scheme of things. This is a very delicate case and one that needs the utmost finesse."

"Yes, I only did what I deemed to be right," Astrid responded politely.

He was lucky that Samuel was not scolding him any further. He was thankful for such a small mercy, no matter even if it seemed miniscule. Unfortunately, this recalling of events, namely Astrid's stalking of the witch, fell on deaf ears as James was not even remotely impressed with Astrid's conduct, expressing so as he voiced his disapproval.

"Yes, that is all well and good. But we have been dealing with this case for months. This creature is destined for the most inexplicable darkness known on the flurries of the mortal realm and you have a close encounter with her? It compels me to say it, but that could have befallen on you and us with mortifying consequences."

Oh fuck, Astrid motioned in thought. *Is there anything these folk do not have knowledge of? Is there a little bell that those "on high" use to communicate with each other to make their spying so much more fruitful? Just press that little bell and they instantly all know who is doing what and at which time and place.* The raven mocked them sneeringly in thought.

Anyway, let's not focus on that. The "on high" has been delving into this much longer than I can detail. Let's not pursue this anymore. I can't be asked with a confrontation between this guy and Samuel. They have their end in this and I will continue to do what I deem worthy to this great cause. I must make haste in not being caught next time however.

Astrid mused quietly in the realization that if he was going to keep tabs on Isra and for any reason and the "on high" or Samuel didn't advocate to what he was undertaking, Astrid would have to do things in his own way, thus gathering his own intelligence and becoming the lone wolf in this grand mystical scheme of keeping watch on Isra. More accurately, Lady Isra as she was soon to be known.

Astrid paused, wondering what James's role was in all this and why the "on high" had been so damn secretive over the whole charade. Clearly it had been kept under wraps for some time since James had said he had been involved in this for months.

Hmmm, I wonder. Are they really conducting themselves in this highly controlled manner now? I wonder what else they know about me and the witch, Astrid pondered with a worried gaze as James was still eyeballing the raven with ardent curiosity.

But before Astrid could delve into just what this might be or what might be occurring behind the glass door that those "on high" had knowledge of, James callously interrupted him mid thought.

"You know, it would be better if you had no further contact with Isra," James said bluntly to Astrid with no emotion whatsoever.

Astrid was taken aback. *Are you actually serious? What in the heavens? This is absolutely ludicrous. You expect me to stay away from her when I've seen the catalyst that is going to send her hell bound? You have got to be joking, surely? The boys "on high" really didn't give this that much careful thought at all.* Astrid almost exploded with these thoughts surging inside his head.

"I am presuming that is indeed a joke?" Astrid demanded.

It was apparent that the raven was becoming very angry now. After all, he was the one that was originally assigned to come into contact with Isra, and now the "on high" was taking that from him? Oh, he was not best pleased; you could guarantee that if nothing else.

Samuel had observed the opposition that was rife between James and Astrid. The forlorn light warrior sat quietly at his desk unable to do anything but digest the pungently bitter atmosphere that was fiercely developing between Astrid and James. Unfortunately, Samuel knew that Astrid wasn't letting on why he was really grieved at this sudden decision. It was obvious to all and sundry that Astrid had developed somewhat of a fascination with this witch Isra, but Astrid wasn't going to admit that in a hurry. No, he'd drag that out until the very end, being stubborn as he could be, for that was his way.

Samuel knew better than most how Astrid could sink his claws into intoxicating situations and then not be able to remove himself from such atrocities without causing damage to his person. Almost like a person who walked into a dragon's den without comprehending that the creature could kill them before they planned their escape. It gave Samuel the impression that Astrid secretly yearned for the danger and rapturous excitement that came from being enveloped in such transgressions. However, Samuel did extend a lot of sympathy toward Astrid despite his severe and stern approach with him because if anyone knew the inside scoop on Astrid, it was undoubtedly Samuel.

Even from the first moment Samuel had found Astrid wandering around in his supposedly, "cut off from the rest of the world" stronghold, the raven and he had developed a rapport right there and then, the basis of which they had formed a friendship upon, which was that both Samuel and Astrid had witnessed far too much bloodshed and loss in their lives as a result of the darkness taking over lost souls.

Now Samuel was already in the business of bringing light into the lives of those who had sought refuge in the dark. Astrid, on the other hand was more of a solitary personage that stayed close to the shadows, looking in on something rather than being part of it. So Samuel made Astrid the raven an offer. To fight alongside him, for a greater good. To give him a purpose that he may not have otherwise discovered. And thus, Astrid became Samuel's right winged man, or raven as was more accurate.

It was safe to say Samuel held the keys of which to unlock the true facets of who Astrid really was, but now things had changed for the better. Times were not the same now as they were back when he and Astrid had first become acquainted. Darkness was more powerful, having more opportunities to wreak havoc upon the feeble lands and so being in the light was so much more challenging. The fight had become a mission, for more beings were taken over by the twilight as the days dawned on.

With all this in mind, Samuel hatched a plan to switch things around much to the annoyance of his black feathered friend. Samuel felt like Astrid had become too involved with the witch. And if he didn't intervene and stop something catastrophic from happening, then who would? The way he saw it he was just enacting what nobody else had the gusto to do.

"Yes, well I am afraid I have to agree with James on this one, Astrid. You are way too entangled with our witch in question. It is right, what he says, you know. Which brings me to the heart of our arrangement." Samuel coaxed to Astrid, gently explaining the situation.

The heart of it? Is that a sarcastic joke at my expense? Astrid mumbled silently to himself. *I mean really, he couldn't have come up with a better pun than that. Deliberate references to subjects that we most definitely should not be conversing about. Sneaky, I must say!*

Samuel saw the raven Astrid curse to himself, looking like he was absolutely furious with this decision that had been made without his notification. So Samuel being the diplomat he decided to smooth things over a little.

"James has been chosen for a reason. You see, there is much more to this tale than we have let on, dear boy. James is not completely all he seems," Samuel elucidated, taking care to watch Astrid's facial expressions for he was sure all this was succeeding in doing was pissing Astrid off no end. But it was better than lying to him, right?

"Oh, let me guess; he's some prissy pretty boy coming from a privileged land where they all reign in airs and graces. And they dance with unicorns and prance around like fairies." Astrid blurted out his thoughts a little too sarcastically, clearly expressing his opinion like verbal vomit after it had been sprayed all over the vicinity.

"That's enough!" Samuel barked.

The gruffness of his voice was enough to let Astrid know that the light bringer meant business. But still, Samuel had not finished with his harsh deliverance, not just yet. Having barely just about enough tolerance for Astrid's mischievous ways on a good day, the righteous leader was getting rather impetuous over Astrid's lack of respect.

"I'll have you know that callous remarks are not tolerated in my presence, do you hear me? But you will listen to what I have to relay to you. And believe me, if I find out that you have disobeyed me, boy, there will be hell to pay. You know in our domain that could be literally so do not defy me. EVER!" Samuel bellowed, now having seemed to have lost all his patience.

Taking a pause to regain his composure, Samuel reached for a crystalline glass decanter sitting idly on his desk. In a swift motion, Samuel began fiddling around in the drawer beneath him, fishing out a clean glass. Still very much irritated, Samuel slammed the glass on his desk carefully pouring the glossy brown contents of the decanter into it, making no excuses as he chugged the sticky brown whisky down his throat in one fatal hit.

"Ah, you can never go wrong with a glass of ye olde Irish whisky. And now let us resume a more amicable discussion, shall we?" Samuel muttered in Astrid's direction but also maintained eye contact with James who had remained silent during Samuel's stern reprimand. "Firstly, James was chosen for this role because only someone who has knowledge of witches can undertake such a task. He will be on the front-line with Isra, so to speak, learning all he can about what she is and why, and gaining her trust while debunking every last vile and sordid revulsion that sends her to such extreme lengths."

Samuel paused, giving James a subtle wink before addressing Astrid as he continued once more. "It will be perilous to say the least. We can't just have any old peasant going down there with her. This requires finesse, something I am not sure if you possess in this area of expertise," Samuel related with sheer caution, again taking great care to not say something that would greatly offend the raven.

The wise old leader continued. "We must remember to take care, for she is a reckless creature with so much rage inside her already. You say she is consumed with the loss of love and so with this we must take precautions. I cannot allow you to go down there and be in the midst of it when it comes full circle, Astrid. You must understand my reasoning is not to punish you for your misgivings. On the contrary, actually," Samuel remarked with great importance, emphasizing the need for vigilance and making it painstakingly known how great the danger could be.

"You will be involved in this mission, for you know more than anyone else how important our work is in these matters. It will be under my complete supervision, of course. We cannot allow for any casualties, supposing it goes down as dire as it has been foretold," Samuel added in swiftly before turning to James with a furrowed brow.

After this acknowledgment, Samuel took a moment to wipe a few escaping beads of sweat from his forehead with a white silk handkerchief before getting back to the topic of concern. This conversation had been exhausting for Samuel and although it had been back breaking to tell Astrid such a brutal truth, at least he had done it. Samuel did not believe in coaxing anyone with a beautiful lie. It was not considered an adequate way to operate in the business of fighting dark foes. You were either truthful with your comrades, or you were booted out before someone could say, "Discrepancy."

"Anyhow, we are finished here," Samuel concluded in earnest fashion, glancing at his whisky decanter favorably as he pondered the idea of helping himself to another glass.

A little swig won't do me harm. After all, it has been a rather tiresome evening! Samuel consoled himself in his thoughts. Finally with James taking control of things on his end, Samuel could have a much needed rest. Or at least one hoped that would be the case.

Astrid remained sullen, having been kept abreast with the intrinsic details of what was going on underneath his wing. However, a question happened to pop up which caused him to become a tad skeptical of the proceedings. But if you don't ask, how can you ever grasp what it is that you don't have a hold on?

"Something has come to my mind which makes me feel quite the enquirer," Astrid motioned bravely, succumbing to his idle curiosity.

"Go on," Samuel urged, never being one to discourage someone from discerning their form of truth.

"I have to say I find all this rather bemusing. You act as though she is a venomous soul but yet I have been in close proximity to her and have observed nothing of that nature. If you please, I would like to know why you think so?" Astrid requested in a gracious manner.

Samuel could only wink at his protégé with his subliminal reply.

"Let's just say some things can only be seen with the eye and not the heart, my boy. Trust me; it will all become clear in time."

Astrid nodded his head in agreement that his question had been most deftly answered.

"If you don't mind, I will take my leave. I feel like trying my luck for a tasty earthworm or two. I know it is almost midnight but I might be fruitful in my search if I happen to take flight now," Astrid replied as he found the need to excuse himself.

"Go fill your stomach. I expect it has been depleted for quite some time while we have been talking," Samuel responded with a smile.

"Thank you, Master," Astrid acknowledged, giving Samuel a low bow before departing through the thick blue velvet curtain before someone could utter another word.

Samuel waited for a moment, eyeing James up and making haste to say absolutely nothing while pressing a cautious finger toward his lips as if to signal James to be silent just for the moment. As time passed, Samuel kept an ear out to listen to the goings on of the outside world, for Astrid would be heard exiting through the creaking oak door at any second now. *Slam* it went from downstairs as it shut, clearly letting the rest of the world know that Astrid had surged into oblivion.

"Okay, now we know he has left the premises, so let's get real here," Samuel remarked as he turned to James with a serious disposition resounding upon his face, clearly depicting there that was something Samuel was not disclosing to Astrid.

Samuel edged in real close, almost practically elbowing James as he whispered in James' ear in a low voice, "Please do not ever reveal to Astrid what we both know. He would not take it well."

James merely smiled but remained formal in his manner as he uttered, "Absolutely, discretion is imperative if we are to win this war!"

"And what a war it will be." Samuel motioned toward James with yet another wink.

16

It was bitterly cold out. The rain hammered down upon the grass soaking every last blade, making the luscious green blades look almost translucent as they glistened in the night's bitter aglow. Anyone would think that winter was due with all the rain that plummeted down, getting heavier with each night. Autumn would soon be depositing its fragrant rich shades of warm orange and blood-red across the land, but first there must be yet another downpour, for summer was not yet done.

Isra, on the other hand, didn't seem to mind the rain. She found its presence quite comforting as it soaked her skin to her weary and fragile bones. The black of her soft velvet cloak was almost glossy as the wet article of clothing clung on to the witch's back making it rigid on her slender figure. But being dripping wet and standing on the edge of nowhere was the very least of Isra's problems.

In all honesty, Isra had ventured far away from the borders of Seclera to a quaint little clearing between some trees in which Isra hoped she wouldn't be disturbed. The last few days had been a nonstop revelation and now she sought peace and clarity. She had a sheer need to make sense of it all and trust me, she could not do that back in Wingdom's.

With Everilda becoming Isra's shadow of late, having any kind of stillness around those parts was virtually impossible. But let's not forget that Isra was her own person. She didn't answer to anyone. She could abscond any time she pleased and this was one of those times. And so she'd disappeared into the night without a soul having any indication of her whereabouts.

It was the perfect reprieve to all this chaos that seemed to come at her ever since she'd learned of Everilda and Jonathan's sordid affair. Not only that, but Isra was also now made aware that Jonathan was under a fateful curse done by the one and only Everilda, all thanks to yet another revelation the universe had chosen to bestow onto Isra, and who could blame her for feeling so desolate after so much upheaval commencing in her life in just a few days?

Isra stood out in the rain on the most perilous of nights. She could have chosen to make her departure, but still ... needs must, right? The air was clear despite the harsh winds and torrent precipitating all around her. Ironic when you consider that she'd come out to escape the roughness of the world that she was doomed to live in, but let's not dwell on the negative.

"At least out in this wilderness I can finally collect my thoughts," Isra muttered to herself out loud, presuming that she wasn't going to be overheard. "After so much heartache and grievances, I hope to be able to rectify some of the pieces of my lost and wandering heart. Perhaps have an understanding of why this has occurred. I'd like to discern the nonsensical from the cold hard truth, if such a thing is possible."

Suddenly, she heard something coming from behind the trees. A rustling sound appeared to be growing closer as Isra swung her head side to head and glanced behind her. *That's strange. I didn't think anyone was here. It's the dead of night so who could possibly be in this quaint forestry place that I've chosen to hide away in? Hmm.*

She'd almost lost track of what she had been thinking about previously as she was now terribly distracted by such an intrusion, but before Isra could ponder any further, a voice sounded out in the distance.

"Hello Isra," Everilda purred, peeking from beyond the tree. Everilda's blonde hair appeared slightly matted with a yellowish sheen, wet from the rain.

Everilda stared over at Isra as she was standing in a blue velvet cloak that was saturated from the downpour. The blueness of it almost blended in with the cobalt-blue sky which might have made Isra giggle had she not been so irritated with Everilda coming after her in this manner. After all, their last meeting was far from pleasant.

Isra folded her arms in a defensive stance, clearly abhorrent to Everilda's untimely visit. And how immaculate her timing was since Isra was considering her place in the scheme of things in such a dramatic way. You know, this was such a dreary world that Isra inhabited and she was honestly wondering whether she fit into it.

"What the hell are you doing here, Everilda?" Isra called out to her foe bluntly. Isra was making it unambiguous that there wasn't going to be a single ounce of jovial interaction here.

Everilda only shrugged her shoulders but yet had the biggest grin upon her face like she was about to gloat over something. It appeared as if she had come here to rub even more salt into the ever-expanding wound open between her and Isra, as if there wasn't enough of that already, but if you knew Everilda well enough, you'd know that there was never a limit with her on these things.

"I thought we should clear a few matters up," Everilda voiced earnestly.

To the common observer it would have appeared genuine the way Everilda remained close to the shadows with the grin that she had painted on her face. She also seemed to have some composure in her stance, but of course Isra would have none of it.

She responded with a huffy, "Hmm."

"Isra, I understand you are aggrieved but I mean you no malice." Everilda spoke coherently with very little aggression in her voice. It was as though she was almost being diplomatic.

Isra said nothing, being defiant in her silence which seemed to rile Everilda a little as she crossed her arms to match Isra's defensive stance. However, Everilda was more laid back than Isra, having already possessed the power to push the younger witch's buttons.

Everilda would have to take a very different approach in order to get through to Isra, but how? It was evident to all that could view such a debacle that was taking place in the dead of the night that Isra was very angry toward Everilda, and who could blame her? But Everilda needed to get Isra on her side if she was going to succeed in the next phase of her plan.

I'm not done here. She won't respond to my reasoning, well heck, I'll have to try something a little more elaborate. Our Isra is so stubborn. My goodness. I just have to get her around to my way of thinking, but how to do it? Manipulation? No, I've tried that and it failed miserably. Jonathan? No. That enactment was a total loss too. Now what can I do? Everilda mumbled to herself callously in thought.

Of course, Isra was not as worldly as Everilda was, which ultimately gave the fair-haired witch the advantage if one knew how to correctly use that to get what she needed.

Hmm, I must be imperative about this. I can't allow for any more blunders because that would be truly embarrassing on my behalf. Now, there must be something. Isra is still a virgin, is she not? There must be something about her purity that I can use to exploit her. Damn it, this is harder than I had presumed. Must try harder, Evie. One must always attempt to conquer that which seems unattainable on the surface. Remember what mother used to say, never say never, Everilda continued to herself as she struggled to think of a way to win over Isra.

It hadn't seemed this complex when she'd sat in her quarters, dreaming up the perfect plan. Everilda had thought it all out so well. She'd have deemed it all out to be Jonathan's fault as far as Isra was concerned, and that he had set out to make Everilda his while also keeping Isra on the sidelines. Both seemed to make him ruthless and cunning as he pitted both friends against one another in a cataclysmal fury that would only succeed in having them both at each other's throats.

Yes, that did seem to have potential, but now Everilda was ranking in front of Isra. The two of them were face to face in what seemed like a battle of wits and suddenly it did not appear so straight forward.

Maybe I should change tact? After all, she's not exactly someone who will hear me out on this unless I really appeal to her good nature. But how can I accomplish that? I've made haste in doing so many things already and nothing has worked. Oh to hell with it. I'm just going to do this my way and if she bites, well I'm onto a winner, Everilda mused sardonically in her thoughts. An evil smile resounded upon her face as though she was suddenly victorious.

"Come on, girl. You and I are better than this. We became friends almost instantaneously. I know there have been injustices committed in my wake, but please listen to what I have to say, if only for a moment and then you can tell me to go on my merry way, but you must hear my side of it," Everilda compelled Isra in a sweetened yet amicable voice almost as though she was doing her utmost to convince Isra that this barrel of subterfuge was indeed genuine, especially as she smiled at her former friend just to add to the bullshit she was spreading.

Isra didn't seem to be convinced by the tale Everilda was spinning. Her glowing green eyes narrowed across at Everilda as if scrutinizing her for any signs of deception. But Isra lowered her cloak to reveal her almost dry chocolate-brown hair that in the night's cover appeared more hazel in tone as her curls descended in ringlets. However, Isra's eyes were still affixed to Everilda, clearly not caring how viscous she looked, and all Isra gave Everilda was a deafening quiet that she presumed the other witch could not bear since Everilda began shifting around uncomfortably, looking to the side and back of her as though she was awaiting an attack of some kind.

No, Isra was not giving Everilda any indication of how she truly felt, almost stringing along her foe in a sense while Isra tried to decipher what was make believe and what was truth. And the best part was Everilda hadn't even given her version of events concerning the ill-fated Jonathan as of yet. Surely, she was saving the best until last? Because there was telling a tall tale and then there was not being able to distinguish the truth from fiction because you've spun such an elaborate web of lies in a weak attempt to conceal the ugly truth.

"Yes, we were friends," Isra muttered. "But you put paid to that by taking my man, someone who I believed truly wanted me for the person I am and yet you just couldn't help yourself. You had to snatch him away from me."

Isra recoiled bitterly. You could almost taste the sourness from her as it emitted off her tongue. She was so angry about the whole charade, and could you honestly expect anything else? Isra was the wronged party here. She wasn't just heartbroken. Isra was also very much in mourning as she appeared dressed from head to toe in black. The somber look that one would own when they were widowed, their loved one having left them to ditch this reality for another plane of existence.

Everilda didn't really have much in the way of a defense for her actions as she replied, "Yes, well needs must. It happened. I can't really do much about it now, can I?"

Isra suddenly looked at Everilda in a new light, almost though there was something startling emerging. She hadn't considered all the factors in this third-party situation between herself, Everilda, and of course Jonathan. But now there was a new dawn. A light bulb had been switched on inside the mechanisms of Isra's brain in a sense, as on a spur of the moment. For the first time since Everilda and Isra had become mortal enemies, Isra smiled, chuckling to herself.

Stupid girl. Isra laughed at once inside herself for now she was pondering something that had not been made clear in its entirety this whole time. *Even at your best, I can still overrule you. And the most satisfying part? I never saw this coming.*

Isra straightened her stance, smoothing out some of her wet, brown, sodden hair as she met Everilda's eyes in a dead stare. "No, but I can," Isra mouthed in a sinister voice, one that could only sound evil no matter how Isra had uttered those words.

Everilda was immediately taken aback by this. The fair-haired witch trembled as her feet struggled to remain steady on the drenched forest floor.

What in glorious damnation does she mean by that? Oh, please don't tell me she's thought of a novel way to solve our predicament of sorts. I hadn't prepared for this at all, Everilda thought at once. *Oh, good golly! I don't even know what she's thinking. She's so much more advanced than me in all aspects of magic. Oh heavens! What am I going to do?* Everilda conversed to herself in a panic.

Now very flighty as she almost began to pace around in a circle, she remembered that Isra was only a few feet away and this would look most suspicious. The last thing Everilda wanted to do was give her enemy any kind of ammunition because she was sure Isra would seize the opportunity to use it against her.

Everilda had to get smart and fast if she was going to achieve anything. To get out of this downtrodden mess that she had sunk right into, Everilda was going to have to be something she never imagined in a million light years. Everilda was going to have to be nice. It was the thing the older witch detested with a passion but nevertheless, needs did really must on this occasion.

"Forgive me, girl, but what does that mean?" Everilda asked Isra earnestly, or at least trying to sound somewhat pleasant in her manner.

Any weakness Everilda showed now would surely be detected. She could tell just by the way Isra's emerald green eyes shimmered back and forth almost alive in the sense that something was beguiling Isra in a marvelous and yet intriguing way.

Isra held all the cards. Everilda had none whatsoever to play. She was well and truly doomed whichever way she looked at it. And to think Everilda had come out here in such terrible terrain to one up Isra in some way. Ha, what a failure that had turned out to be.

Isra remained defiant, only smiling at Everilda. An applied grin that was plastered on her face as if she was aware of something that Everilda clearly had not considered gave Everilda the apparent notion that Isra wasn't so concerned with the sadness of her betrayal any longer. Oh no, that sly grin revealed something else entirely. It screamed revenge. A brutal and hardcore act of malice that only Isra could bestow to its rightful owner, Everilda.

"It means," Isra started with yet another smile, only highlighting her glee a little bit more. "That I have taken stock of our little arrangement and I failed to take into account the seriousness of your crime," Isra responded calmly, showing no sign of anger which only made Everilda more worried.

Everilda's glossy blue eyes didn't resemble the sky any longer, for they were full of fear, no longer that perfect shade of blue. The color had drained right out of them. Everilda looked very much washed out. Ironic when you consider that Everilda was a clandestine copy that had come from a long line of powerful witches, mostly stemming from her father's end. But no, she was now feeling very weak indeed.

"You see, when I look at how I've reacted to this shindig between you and Jonathan, I realized something..." Isra motioned, still being as cool as a cucumber. "I've been tearing about the place crying, weeping. Doing all the wrong things, acting as if I'm the victim here, when actually we both know who is going to sit up on the throne of victim mentality. Don't we, Everilda?" Isra cooed.

"And it pains me to see you suffering in this way," Isra continued. Now the venom was exploding out of Isra's mouth, oozing up from her throat like blood that had run cold. "I cannot allow any more gratifications to your person," Isra said coolly in a most cryptic voice.

She was not giving any leeway to Everilda or revealing any fragment of her plan which could only add to Everilda's anguish.

"I see," Everilda responded frostily. She made it apparent she was not happy to be beaten, but what other option was there to be found?

Isra was clearly triumphant, especially when you factored in that Isra was not letting on to anything in regard to how she was executing her plan.

"Anyway, *needs must*," Isra concluded with a snide grin, letting her fateful foe know that this conversation was well and truly over.

"Yes, I can see that," Everilda finished in a hushed tone, for now it was clear nothing she was going to say would sway Isra to her way of thinking.

It was far too late for that. Isra had her own agenda and much to Everilda's anguish it was going to rival her own shifty plan knocking it on its head, metaphorically speaking, anyhow. All Everilda could do was stand back in utter amazement as Isra swiftly dissipated amongst the tall trees with her black, soaking wet cloak trailing behind her. The only clue that she was still lingering within the forest also disappeared after a moment.

Yes, needs truly must, Everilda thought to herself as she felt totally crushed, not having any leverage to fool Isra that there still could be some kind of accord between them both.

Everilda's grand plan to throw all manner of blame onto Jonathan hadn't been given a premise to start with so now she was destined to fail unless she suddenly came up with a better way to take down Isra. And if Everilda did have any means in subduing Isra, she'd better do it fast or she'd be a dead duck.

EVERILDA SAT upon her red couch twiddling her thumbs as she was restless. Her blonde hair hung down by her face in a matted mess and she was over thinking every last segment of the last few days. In just the space of a couple of days, Everilda and Isra had gone from being fond friends to mortal enemies and Everilda was almost out of time.

There was no way to salvage that friendship. It was gone, withered and burned away. Everilda's betrayal with the ill-fated Jonathan had sealed the deal there, causing Isra to turn her back on Everilda. And some would say that Isra was doing all she could to perform a perfectly exacted revenge on her former companion. All that you had to see was the body language Isra exhibited whenever in fleeting distance of Everilda to know that she was mad, seething, and incredibly bitter as nothing but resentment and hatred was all that remained between the two of them.

So it really wasn't an understatement to say that Everilda was quaking in her fine black leather boots. She had gone over and over it all in her head, trying to piece together how on earth she was going to come back from this. The uncertainty of not knowing what Isra was going to do certainly was troubling for Everilda. This only made her impending sense of doom even more terrifying as she sat practically rocking herself on her couch since she came back to her apartment at Wingdom's.

Everilda raised her eyes upward at the ceiling denoting the silence that originated from the level above her own desolate home, the exact same floor in which Isra's quarters were situated which did little to comfort Everilda in her time of distress as it only confirmed that Isra was still out there somewhere in these wild winds. Otherwise Everilda presumed she'd have heard Isra come back by now.

"Well, she's out there stomping her fury across the lands and goodness knows what she will do," Everilda murmured quietly to herself in pursuit of the idea that Isra was really out for blood. "But hang on a minute, where does Jonathan fit into this? I mean, she must hold him responsible too, right? I can't be the person that gets all the blame laid upon them, surely?" Everilda had actually forgotten Jonathan amidst all the chaos with Isra brewing a storm.

Jonathan. Ah yes, him. That spineless, despicable excuse for a man. What else could be said about him? He wasn't exactly the boldest of fellows having tried to weasel out of Isra finding out about Everilda and himself, but Everilda wasn't dense. She had made deftly sure Isra had found out by shouting the odds with Jonathan right outside Wingdom's. How novel of her to pick that as the prime location to lay into Jonathan. It was genius really when you took time to think about how well that little shindig was designed by none other than Everilda.

As for Jonathan, Everilda was perusing going to see him. It wasn't that far from the borders of Seclera and Spirisity although she had no inclination that any such land existed, but having been to Jonathan's dreary hovel many times before, she knew exactly where he would be. Hiding from the world no doubt. And with Isra out gallivanting across the horizon somewhere plotting revenge, Everilda truly believed that was a good policy even for a cowardly loser like him.

Still, needs must, the witch thought to herself, suddenly

conjuring up a plan. She would visit Jonathan in his homely terrain, a place where he'd be at ease and unsuspecting of what was coming, and then she'd lay it all out for him. Oh baby, this wasn't going to be pretty because when Everilda started dishing out a few home truths of what things really were beyond the sidelines, there was the potency for things to get really messy.

"Yes, I'll go see that miserable prick. Tell him off good and proper, I shall. Bet he might fancy me a little more than Isra after this," Everilda chuckled to herself, wondering why she hadn't thought of this little scenario beforehand. "I am so stupid. I came up with everything but trapping Jonathan right in the middle. Just where did my brain wander off to? It must have been dazed with all this worry of what Isra was cooking up. Well, let's see how clever and cunning she is after this," Everilda said as the realization became stronger with every moment she sat with her lips pursed.

"Oh Isra, dear sweet Isra. You thought you could befall me with your conniving treachery, but even I can teach you a thing or two. Ha!" Everilda cackled merrily with the snidest grin she could ever have mustered.

Now it was time to put her plan into action. Jonathan was about to have an uninvited guest, one he couldn't throw out as Everilda was more than a match for that wretched mortal man. Ha, she could be victorious against him any day.

Well after all, he was under her spell.

17

Although the rain had finally stopped after several hours of torrential showers saturating the grassy plains from where the clouds burst out into the heavens, it was still gloomy where Isra was. Having spent the night sheltered inside a large crevice of a lonely gray mountain peak, it was very much dark for her despite the fact that dawn had surged across the mainland.

Since Isra was veiled inside by the stone accompaniment and away from the world around her, she was in a safe zone. However unbeknownst to her, Isra was not as alone as she had estimated herself to be.

Astrid the raven unfurled his black silky wings, shaking off some stray drops of rain water that had got on them as he had passed the night perched above Isra's isolated hiding place. How he had managed to catch up with her and find out where she had absconded to during the small hours in such horrific weather conditions one would not know. Although it had to be said that Astrid did have a knack for staking out the witch.

It was somewhat amusing that Isra had not caught him since he was literally above the mountain peak in which she had chosen to hide. But in all fairness, Isra's mind was elsewhere. Hence why she had sought refuge in this derelict crevice far away from the borders of Seclera and any coordinates she had ever known.

In fact, Isra had no inclination of where she was, exactly. She knew she had been in the forest since having ventured far and wide just to get away from the lavish Wingdom's Academy and having found sanctuary amongst the trees, but where she was now, she had no clue. After leaving Everilda marinating in her trepidation and fury at having not won out in their blasted confrontation, Isra decided that she didn't need to just run from the borders of Seclera. Oh no, she'd have to be a lot more thorough and go somewhere that no soul would think to look for her. And it would have been presumed clever for the witch if she had any idea of where she had ended up.

The mountain peak didn't have much going for it. Dull gray coloring reminded Isra hilariously of the creepy gargoyle statues of Wingdom's that resembled the actual life-like imagery of demons. But other than that, it was tall, narrow; and despite the fact that it appeared to be withering away with each passing sunrise, it seemed to be quite the sturdy structure. Of course, there was no danger of the cliff face breaking off and collapsing on top of Isra. Well, that would be quite the sticky ending for her, wouldn't it?

But it did beg the question of why this area was so deserted, indisputably not having been inhabited for hundreds of years. One could ponder the idea of what might have taken place in these lonely plains for it to become such an abandoned relic, a bleak eyesore that had clearly been left behind in favor of something more appealing in design. Nevertheless, the guise of the mountain peak was not to be sniffed at, for it reeked of magic within those humble stone walls.

Anyone who was even remotely inclined would be able to decipher the true lineage of whatever or whomever had caused all manner of grotesque havoc here, and Isra was no exception.

Isra was curious after an hour or so of staring at the gray stone peaks in her awakening stage, and she decided she simply couldn't resist the temptation of them any longer. She rubbed the sleep from her eyes and poked her head out from the crevice, checking that the coast was clear and that no eyes were on her. Of course, if she had only looked above her, she'd have discovered a very yellow sheen gold pair of eyes in the form of Astrid, but she had not yet discovered him scrutinizing her every move, much to his relief.

Tearing herself away from the crevice, Isra walked over to the gray peaks situated only a minute away from her person. This idealistic land cut off from any possible known being that she could sniff out was perfect for her grand scheme in thinking of how to take down Everilda. For Isra was very angry with her former friend. And it wasn't justice enough seeing Everilda sweat. Oh no, there was much more fun to be had here, and Isra wasn't going to be satisfied until she had it.

However, Isra wasn't completely adapted to the darker aspects of magic. The unknown and forbidden arts that the joyous folk at Wingdom's didn't care teach any of their young witches, that is. That stuff was almost deadly in the wrong hands, and right now, Isra definitely slotted into the category one would fit into if they really wanted to create a stir with the most horrific magics on this earth. She was out for revenge with a destructive yearning for darkness to boot.

Isra glanced at the gray stone peak for a moment almost in wonder as she really wanted to know just what lay within that solid foundation. So while pondering this notion for a few transcendent moments almost as if she was in a trance, Isra pressed her hand against the exalted structure. Only the impact that followed, not a soul could have predicted.

Immediately, a glowing lime green light burned around Isra's hand surging around her as her hand came into contact with the mountain peak, so powerful it created a rupture from inside the mountain causing the entire precipice to shake violently. Astrid was perched right on top of the eminence so imagine the raven's sheer horror when he felt it convulsing from underneath him.

"What the fuck?" Astrid called out as the mountain shook

continuously, forcing him to sink his claws into the gray stone just to get a grip on reality as he knew it.

Astrid forced himself to look down despite the vertigo he was experiencing that almost caused his stomach to force up that delightful snack of worms he'd had earlier. That certainly would not have been pleasant. Scanning the scene before him with his gold shimmery eyes, Astrid quickly realized he was close to Isra catching sight of him. It would only take one false move and he would be exposed. Samuel would not be amused at his actions.

"Shit!" Astrid gasped, already feeling the close proximity between himself and the witch. One slip of a claw and he'd be on the floor in front of her, but oddly enough, Astrid was more preoccupied with what Isra was doing at the mountain's edge. "What in the heavens is she doing???"

The raven cawed ferociously as he felt Isra's energy connect with the potent darkness that lingered from within the mountain. It was intense, that was for sure. The raven felt Isra's strong energy coming up from above and Astrid suspected it was only going to get worse.

"I need to move from here. Now!" Astrid commanded himself knowing he had to get out of here as fast as his wings would take him.

But then there was a pause. A deafening silence filled the air as a sense of foreboding surrounded the raven. Dread. Lingering fear. It penetrated across the entire spot where Isra was, almost covering her in its pernicious stench as the whole area smelled of burnt molten lava.

"Oh, this can't be good at all. Destined for darkness and she's out here having up close and personal relations with the most ghastly energies that have been forbidden for eons!" Astrid croaked somberly.

The raven admonishing that he knew exactly what was sealed up away from any impertinent minds in these hallowed walls confirmed that it was indeed outlawed. One would probably wonder how Astrid knew of this mountain's history and why it was deemed so treacherous to all who dared seek it.

"I must get back to Samuel immediately," Astrid advised himself.

Only before Astrid even had the chance to stretch his wings to take off into the warm morning skies that would surely blind him with their candy corn-orange sunlit rays, James materialized in front of him with a flash. Stood before Astrid with a vagrant sneer, his eyes met with the raven's in a disturbing yet snide manner.

"Ha. I caught you!" James jeered at Astrid.

"Caught me what? You do realize our witch Isra is right underneath this very cliff top. You do know that, right?" Astrid hollered at James, clearly not interested in why James was here upon the shaking mountain but more concerned with the matter at hand: not being caught by Isra, because then all would be lost.

"Is there really no end to your stalking?" James chided at Astrid. James smirked at Astrid, evidently very pleased that had managed to catch the raven in such an awkward state of disarray.

"If you don't mind, you might want to take a look below us!" Astrid looked down toward Isra, hoping James would follow his eyes to where she was still standing.

"Ah yes, I can fix that," James muttered.

And with one swift movement of two fingers from James, Isra was frozen stiff as was the scene around her including the potent green magic. The entire mountain peak and everything surrounding it had been magically halted in time leaving just Astrid and James able to have full mobility in the empty wasteland. Astrid was not amused by this gesture, having already had enough of James from their meeting with Samuel. The raven launched a verbal attack at the human, almost spitting with his eyes locked in rage that he had wanted to express since the previous night.

"You know I could peck your eyeballs out now, gobbling them up like a salivating morsel, leaving not one scrap of evidence for anyone to know you were ever here!" Astrid squawked at James in a beseeched tone.

"Ha! And Samuel would be really chuffed with that move. You'd be banished from the lands before you could even utter the word 'peasant'!" James snapped back at the raven.

"Yes, well, whatever," Astrid continued, clearly realizing this was not a battle he was going to win. There would have to be some kind of compromise especially if he was going to succeed in not being punished by Samuel. "What the hell are you even doing here?" Astrid asked James in a sullen voice tinged with suspicion, for the raven did not trust the human James.

"I could ask you the same thing. Does the word 'forbidden' escape your dimwitted vocabulary?" James provoked Astrid, undoubtedly being sarcastic to really ruffle Astrid's feathers.

"Oh. That. Well..." Astrid began although he realized he couldn't actually confess to James why he was watching Isra in this strange yet transfixed manner in which he had practically become her shadow in recent weeks. So it was best for Astrid to throw James off the scent, avoiding the issue entirely because it was obvious he had been caught anyway, so what point was there in denying it?

"Never mind. You know why I'm here. You've caught me. So off with you. Go and run back to Samuel, you big tattletale," Astrid countered, equally as sarcastic in flavor. "Pesky humans and their ridiculous humanized ways. Be gone!" Astrid huffed to James, deliberately not looking James in the eye for he was well and truly narked off with him.

"I'm not going to run back to Samuel, as you put it. I'm here for the same reasons as you," James professed in a formal voice as if he were addressing a child, almost another way to royally piss Astrid off, no doubt.

"But you, although your intentions are good, are way too involved with this. You've taken the job a little too seriously, don't you think?" James muttered in the raven's direction. "You are not supposed to be within fleeting distance of Isra, and here I catch you right above her, and not to mention this chaos she's about to unleash. What the fuck were you thinking? Are you really that dense?" James shouted avidly, annoyed while also wondering where Astrid's rationality was in relation to Isra.

"But forget that. I'm supposed to be prim and proper in Samuel's eyes. If he had found out I had scolded you in such an unprofessional manner, he'd surely have my head, metaphorically, anyhow. Let's strike a bargain. You don't tell him about me. And I won't tell him I've seen you here."

James paused for a second, upon the notion that something was missing from his gloriously sarcastic response. "Oh, and for the record, I'm not human. Not strictly speaking anyway!"

He chortled at Astrid with a smug smile as if he was impressed with himself for adding it in there, making haste to unfreeze Isra so she had mobility again, once more resuming the self-inflicted chaos around her.

"You have quite the affinity for our Isra. One might go as far to say you have some kind of love for the girl," James commented as Astrid knew he was exactly right, but the raven was darned if he was going to succumb to admitting it.

Some precious parcels of knowledge were for his beady eyes only. Nobody else even deserved to get a glimpse of what revolved around his mind and heart as far as he was concerned. That was his private business. So what if he loved Isra? It's not like they'd ever have a chance of making a go of things with him being a raven and her, well ... technically still human for now. But unless something happened that would significantly alter the way of things, their union was going to be halted before it even began.

Astrid gave an equally smug grin, snidely chucking to himself as he retorted, "Well, I knew that. I could smell it off you for miles. Nice coloring you have there, young fella. I bet that skin is somewhat tight on you." Astrid was almost hinting that James wasn't accustomed to his human guise while also cleverly changing the subject of conversation.

"Anyway, things are going to be quite perilous around here, so let's shuffle off while we still have all our parts attached, hmm?" James perused, patting his shoulder and inviting the raven to jump on.

Astrid snorted at the idea for a moment but then considered that James might have a point. Not a soul could stop Isra if she had laid her hands on such tainted magics and the best option was to stay out of harm's way while she committed treason against the name of the light. And thinking about it more deeply, Astrid considered that it could be an opportunity to discover more about the unscrupulous James as he was quite the unorthodox character. To be honest, it only compelled Astrid to speculate over just what kind of critter or brute James was rumored to be.

But only time would tell, for the inscrutable James was not giving any indication as to his origins.

18

Everilda rapped her fists upon Jonathan's cottage door while she stood looking around, fearing she could be seen at any moment. She had her long black velvet cloak on and was hoping she'd gotten here in time, for Isra was sure to give Jonathan a timely visit.

If she hasn't been here already and castrated the poor man, or lack thereof, Everilda thought menacingly to herself. *But needs must, we can't allow minor matters to get in the way of business, can we?*

"Oh, come on boy," Everilda cursed in frustration as still no Jonathan.

This was most peculiar as Everilda had suspected he would have answered by now. All right, maybe another tap will do it, this time rapturous and full of the winds of fury. An exceptional pun when you considered that Isra was likely to be full of both.

Rap. Bang!

Everilda's fist pounded against the weak door frame, almost giving the illusion just from the sound alone that it would splinter into pieces just at the malevolent force she had used. She had to, for the poor simpering fool wasn't answering.

JONATHAN STIRRED from inside the darkened hovel that was his living area. A slight patch of drool from where he had dribbled away his most illicit fantasies was on his shirt. Jonathan opened his eyes horrified, for suddenly he had been awoken by the most torturous sound. Upon lifting himself up from the dirty old beige couch of his, he realized it was his front door.

But who in the devil could be knocking at this unsightly hour? It was close to midnight. Who would even want to show up at his doorstep at any time, never mind this unsightly one.

Jonathan was still groggy from his delirious dream where he had been standing in an orchard just above an exquisite raspberry tree brimming with bright pink juicy raspberries. And so yearning for the taste of that succulent satiable fruit, he had extended his hand out to reach it, only much to his disappointment he grasped a raspberry in his hand only to feel something sticky and wet on his palm. Opening his hand, Jonathan saw the raspberry had imploded, gushing with rancid lime-green goo.

"Ewww," he screamed out. "It's tainted. It's rotten. Not fit for consumption."

So he had thrown it onto the ground, mercilessly trying to get the horrid green liquid off his hand in a frenzy, and then he had woken up to the shattering pounding of Everilda's fists. Still not fully coherent, Jonathan forced himself off the beige couch in a feeble attempt to answer the door. Moving stiffly, he walked over to the foyer in which he fumbled around for a candle, only to realize he had not lit any before falling into a slumber.

Rap! The door sounded again, indicating that whoever was awaiting him was getting impatient.

"I am coming. Calm your heels," Jonathan shouted as he felt around the door's edge for the iron latch and bolt that he'd slid across to unlock the door. It felt like he was fiddling with it for ages until he finally found it in the dark.

"About frigging time!" Everilda announced, barging her way into

Jonathan's cottage much to his bemusement. All he could do was stand there taken aback as she let herself into his living area.

"Hurry now. There is much to discuss." Everilda patted the seat on the couch for Jonathan to sit down upon in a demanding fashion.

Jonathan remained standing, not sure what on earth was happening as he glanced at Everilda from the foyer. His eyes were all over her person as if he was cross examining her, searching for whatever bullshit would come flooding from her lips.

"I don't have time for games, Jonathan. Please do sit," Everilda cautioned him in a low voice. Her eyes glared at him in a sense as she appeared very much annoyed with him.

"What the hell are you doing here, Everi?" Jonathan cajoled her, rushing into the living area. However, he refused to sit down. He didn't have any intent of being near the feisty fair-haired witch.

Oh no. She's full of tricks, that one. I'm not falling for that again. I've seen enough of her glamorous flair to last me several centuries, Jonathan cursed to himself in thought, having already been tricked by Everilda to show up at Wingdom's when Everilda had immaculately set it up for none other than Isra to witness the whole kerfuffle as he and Everilda were arguing.

"Yes, she's a sly old dog," he muttered in unison under his breath. "Wonder what elaborate trick she will pull out of the bag this time?"

"Niceties will be very much appreciated, Jonathan. You must remember your place. You are not ruling on the top. You are downtrodden. Face down in the muck." She unleashed a spike of venom emitting from her as if she was bursting like a overwhelmed volcano under so much pressure it was about to burst into flame.

Everilda was an evil soul and was not going to be at peace with him or herself until she'd had her one taste of bitter-sweet revenge. Even if she could make him recoil and want to crawl up and die for one insatiable moment, it would be enough.

I'm going to make him sweat until he's dripping in his own bodily fluids. It's not enough just to frighten him. Oh no, I want him terrified of Isra's very existence. Shaking in his manly skin, or not so, depending on if people view him as a man or a mouse, Everilda mocked to herself with a laugh, for she had always enjoyed emasculating Jonathan. It was one of her favorite pastimes. *I mean, she may not even be coming here for him, but perhaps I can give him the idea that she is. You know, have a little fun with the boy. I have nothing else to occupy my time with. Let's have a bit of extracurricular entertainment to liven up my dull night,* Everilda mused to herself in thought with a gleeful smile.

"Isra is on the warpath, dear," Everilda began in a muted tone, emphasizing the insincerity in her voice. She wanted to make a real meal out of this, giving Jonathan the impression that things were far more worse than he had presumed them to be. "She could be on her merry way this minute to kill you, boy. This is a serious matter. Life and death, so please do take it seriously. I mean, she could castrate you!" Everilda suggested wickedly, unable to hide the smile from her face for just the mere idea of it gave her immense pleasure.

"Kill me? For what?" Jonathan stuttered, still refusing to seat himself next to Everilda. *No, she's full of malice and wicked treachery. Heck, I don't even want her up here in my humble abode. Goodness knows what she will let loose next,* Jonathan thought to himself, petrified of what Everilda would come up with next. Unable to look her in the eyes or even give her a fleeting stone-cold glance from across the room, he remained standing in his own home, practically trembling on her words.

"Isra can't see past irrational thinking right now. She's out for blood. Hell, boy, she'd probably relish the idea of having your still beating heart ripped out from your body while she's stood there laughing," Everilda hinted, turning up the heat just a tiny bit more.

Oh, this is too enjoyable for words. I'm savoring every last moment, Everilda snickered to herself in another highly amusing thought.

"But don't worry, because I'm here. I'll save your scrawny behind," Everilda chortled, struggling to hold back the rapturous laughter she kept within herself.

Jonathan's face turned from almost frantic at the thought of something dire happening to seriously unimpressed and pissed off with Everilda in seconds.

"Funny, as I don't exactly feel confident in your engagingly willful presence," he snarled at her.

Everilda sniggered as she waved a finger at the timid yet angry little man. "Be that as it may, I am your only friend in this predicament." She added a small pause, hoping that by dragging it out that she'd intensify Jonathan's fear. Everilda swiftly lifted herself from the miserable beige couch, striding up on Jonathan in a bold stance, an act that could only make the human man quiver in yet unanticipated fear. "Isn't it better to have to deal with me than our vengeful Isra?" Everilda probed Jonathan with a snide smile, only emitting more malice and venom as the words danced on her tongue.

"I'd take her any day," Jonathan growled furiously, gritting his teeth at her like a wolf about to chomp down on something that had been irritating him. The frustration was bubbling up inside his fists as he kept them by his sides, but you could see the tension as he kept his hands scrunched up tight.

"Ha! Be careful what you wish for, boy. It may just come upon you!" Everilda bated him with even more fury. It didn't matter how much rage and hatred she tossed at Jonathan. He wasn't rising to the bait.

Why isn't he falling for my conniving trickery? You'd think after cursing his sorry arse he'd be on his hands and knees begging me for salvation, but no. The poor man is not even remotely frightened here. Hmm.

Everilda paused in thought, holding her finger to her lips in hope Jonathan wasn't sensing what she was up to. Not that he could really, as he had no powers to speak of. An advantage in her hands, you could say. Maybe there was something she'd missed?

I know I am not quite adept at my craft yet. Perhaps there is something I have not yet sought out. Yes, an occult book or two hidden away at Wingdom's. Maybe I'll find something worthy of my time because this mortal is not. I'm actually getting tired of him. All his wailing defensiveness and blubbery. Oh, it's so bothersome.

"I think you should rethink that attitude of yours before someone decides to put you in a rather gruesome place," Everilda threatened.

She was standing before him practically emitting saliva out of her mouth at him as she spoke, only further demonstrating her anger.

"Get the hell out of here, Everilda!" Jonathan barked at her, shooting his fingers at her in a violent stance as if to show he was meaning business.

"Oh, silly poor old, you!" Everilda cooed. "I'd love to..." She paused midair as if searching for some ravishing comeback that would one up him totally in this battle of nonsensical conflict. "But remember..." she whispered in his ear. "I own you. Forever."

But there was just one tiny predicament. The bold and brash Jonathan was still under Everilda's fateful spell. So, while he might have seemed confident and even willful to defend himself against her verbal wrath, he had forgotten to note that she had one thing she could always use against him. Magic.

Jonathan was mute as the realization dawned upon him that her words were indeed true. His face went numb. Those once darkened brown chestnut eyes of his almost spilled onto the floor in horror, but when Everilda looked upward, she actually noted that there was something remarkably different about dear, sweet Jonathan. His eyes were as black as coals.

19

Completely unaware of Jonathan and Everilda's little confrontation and probably not even caring, Isra was still attached to the mountain peak in the chaos that she had self-induced unto the world since James had unfrozen her, although she had no knowledge of this either.

The impetuous Isra was glowing a bright luminous green from her head to her toes with the potent energy that surged within her, saturating everything around her person and almost blinding her in a sense as it dripped into her mercilessly. The temptation of the sordid mountain peak had clearly worked its will on her and now Isra was at its beck and call. A servant to the dark seeds would soon be the living entity that she would come to live and breathe, although that was unbeknownst to her at this point in time.

It was marvelous, for all one could see for miles on end was bright neon green. The skies were covered in it as it reached as far as the once white and shimmery clouds, and as you got down to the mountain itself, you could see it was imploding out of the crevice descending straight into Isra. She was absolutely encased in it. There was no way of escape although she didn't look like she was particularly grieved by that notion.

And as the lime green flames in shades of somber golden yellow and the harshest day-glow green, some would say her soul was on fire as it appeared to be around her once pale aura. Not now. The damn thing was ablaze with the fiery green sparks that flew around Isra and the desolate land she was in.

The immensely powerful magic gave Isra great satisfaction as it poured into every part of her, thus allowing the deadly dark energy to consume her until it finally came to a standstill much to her bemusement as she hadn't expected the volcanic flow to ever cease.

But despite this robust gushing of fortitude coming to its end, Isra was a sight to behold as she gleamed in the brightest vibrant luminous green, almost like a beacon of the purest, most beautiful, light; only, the fluorescent entity was not of light. Oh no, it was the damnable variety. The one people would only seek out if they wanted to be entangled with those born straight from the depths of hell.

"Oh, well that was intriguing, I must say," Isra gasped, once more having her hand free as she proceeded to walk away from the elegant structure that she had been accustomed to for so long.

"Hold it. Oh, my goodness." A voice shrieked behind her in terror. A young girl with mahogany-brown hair tinged with hints of burgundy red was waving her arms in the air as if trying to signal someone for help. Only this person was in no danger. She was frantically trying to gain Isra's attention. "Oh my, it was you! You are the cause of the magics being awoken! Goodness gracious!" she exclaimed in shock, putting her hand to her mouth as she realized her outburst might come across as rude.

"I didn't do anything," Isra responded quietly.

Isra stopped as she tried to vaguely recall the experience. She had to admit most of it had been a blur. She felt as if she had been cleansed inside out, yet something inside of her was burning which allowed her to know that something tremendously stalwart had collided with her being.

"It called me to it, and then I became enveloped in these cascading rays of green embers as this force field of wondrous power soaked itself into me," Isra explained, although cautious as she had no inclination of who the girl was and more to the point, why she was justifying herself to her.

"Yes. That is darkness for you," the girl answered in a worrisome tone. "It has been forbidden in these parts for many moons now. It was put to slumber by a very resourceful magician that is no longer around to tell his covetous tales. We had thought it was the end of magic of this nature, until you came along and roused the demonic energy."

The girl appeared very frustrated with Isra for some peculiar reason, of which the witch did not know, for all she saw was a young girl barely peaking around sixteen years that was haughty, dressed down in white linen all the way down to her knees where her legs were bare until you got down to the black leather sodden boots that graced her feet.

"Why is it forbidden?" Isra asked with an analytical glance.

It was obvious to all concerned that she was deeply curious as to why folk would shy away from something when there was so much wonder about the land to lay your eyes upon. Surely it was something truly remarkable to be able to seek out the magics and sample their delectable delights, no?

But apparently this strange girl did not believe that was justly so. In fact, as Isra stared into the girl's bewildering grey blueish eyes with a slight tinge of gold about them, she realized there was a little more about this creature than she had anticipated. But what the hell was it?

She was not dark. This girl clearly didn't roam in the shadows awaiting people to fall at her feet as she soaked up the attention recoiling with contorted laughter. No. There was a very different commodity staring Isra in the face here, but she had no inclination of what that might be.

If Isra had the means to do so right now, she'd have been tapping her fingers on her desk as she unraveled the possibility in her mind that this bright young thing was a little bit more than she let on. But then again, Isra had that gift with people, being able to sense what magnificent gifts they possessed deep in their soul and sometimes extravagant bounties of remittance that they had no knowledge of having.

The girl was hesitant as she answered Isra. Her eyes almost fell to the floor as if she was trying to conceal something, but that was near impossible being right in front of Isra even if there was only a small mountain between them.

"It is forbidden because darkness is an entity that can consume and destroy even the sweetest and lightest of beings," the girl responded curtly as though she was addressing a child that had done severe wrongdoing.

"I see," Isra concurred quietly, allowing this to soak into her head, for now something was forming inside her brain, a vibrant image of how things really were when she sunk into her teeth into the reality of this world she had been expelled into. And all because of a sordid betrayal. Isra was so young and still unknowingly naïve, but yet she had that skill to tap into that which surrounded her being.

Isra had been fortunate enough to tap into magics beyond her knowledge and quite conceivably in advance of her adolescence. It was miraculous that Isra had just happened to flee to this quaint old mountain and be lured by these entrancing energies. These enticing forces of gravity compelled her to place her hand against the solid walls of that peak only to be filled with a plethora of power.

That could not have been a coincidence. There had to be some kind of synchronistic deduction as to why that had occurred with her present in its domain. The young girl could see Isra was clearly thinking strategically, having gone into a daydream of sorts as Isra had taken her focus off the girl for a few minutes to converse with herself. However, this silence made the girl feel very uneasy. She didn't like quiet. It always made her feel like something ominous was about to happen.

"Anyway, you should better make haste now. Go on your way before anything else comes out of there." The girl pointed her finger toward the mountain peak's crevice.

"Oh, that?" Isra laughed it off earnestly, mocking the girl with her snide laugh as she evidently found it amusing. "That was rather enthralling. I found it to be very fruitful, although I had come here for a very different reason. Hmm..."

And the witch trailed off again as she remembered she had come to seek counsel of what to do about Everilda. But since then, she had become acquainted with an exuberance of power.

"Oh. Well, I don't know why you sought out this land of all others, but I must warn you that people who come here don't leave the same as they were before," she said in a chilling voice as if she had personal experience of such an entity. "Anyhow, let's lose the awkwardness. It makes me feel complacent. I am Cora," she remarked, taking care to judge how Isra reacted to her friendly manner as she didn't want to offend the green-eyed lady in front of her.

Cora immediately sensed that Isra wasn't exactly the type to be bowled over by strangers, almost as though people riled her a little bit, but she did her best to tolerate them, acting as though they were not there. Cora was someone who was ruled greatly by her heart and just by glancing at Isra with a slightly tense smile Cora could tell that there was something troubling Isra. A very significant event that had led to inner turmoil in her life.

Well, it's no surprise she's found magics to be interesting, really. Whatever has happened, she's hell bent on something. But what it entails, I do not know. I hope I do not find out, Cora mused in thought, clearly paranoid of anything that was slightly unorthodox. Something that might be a little bit off the wall and corpuscular in nature. Anything that could resemble even the slight tinge of darkness.

"I am Isra," Isra replied, unsure of whether she should extend her hand out to beckon a welcoming friendly gesture. She presumed it was likely best to refrain from that.

"Isra, what brings you to our terrain here in Glamvein?" Cora inquired with an impending regard having only just met this transient being, but there was an avid officiousness about Isra that Cora could not help but explore. Perhaps later she would come to realize that this was rather naïve of her, but Cora wasn't the smartest tool in the box.

"I came here to seek refuge from a very dire situation. However, I suddenly feel I have clarity at last. I am sorry, but I must go now. There is a friend of mine awaiting me and I cannot delay her fate any longer," Isra recited solemnly although she had a glint in her eye hinting that her friend's fate was not going to be a pleasant one.

Cora backed away from Isra slightly as those emerald green eyes shone menacingly as though they were ablaze with fiery flames all a flurry with shades of jade green and the slightest tinge of rich yellow. One would begin to question what the devil Isra was up to, but then it was best to refrain from such meddling unless you wanted to get burnt.

"I see. Well nice meeting you, dear soul. Good luck."

Cora bid the formidable Isra goodbye. She had the most auspicious feeling their paths would indeed cross again.

Maybe not in this life. Perhaps the next. But I will see her again, Cora mumbled to herself. *But when that time comes, she will be covered in the dark forces for this creature has already tasted it. She's yearning for more. Dying for the chance to wreak havoc upon those that have wronged her so dreadfully. Ah yes, Isra will be back.*

Cora sensed Isra's shadow side because she was in tune with that of the light and the dark. Having the perfect balance between the two energies, but before you think it was all sweetness and light think again. Cora was under a deadly curse in which she was doomed to fight against those that swayed from the rays of crystalline bliss and there was nothing she could ever do to set herself free.

The poor maiden had not signed up for this, but alas she had a greater calling, something far more imperative than she had deemed it to be for she saw it as a prison and nothing else. Hopefully she would grow to see the deeper purpose that lay within her in time.

20

Everilda sat idly twiddling her shoulder-length blonde hair as she was hunkered upon the famous gray stone steps outside Wingdom's, having left Jonathan's in a fluster as her so-called clever plan had failed her. So much cunningness and agility were all broken down with one poor man using only four words.

So the callous Jonathan had told spiteful Everilda to get out. And good on him, for she was a conniving, snide creature that did her utmost in using him as her pawn in her bitter battle of wits against Isra. However, having failed to accomplish such a feat, she was running out of ideas and also time.

Her grand scheme had all been in vain; well, the whole charade had been for nothing. Everilda had tried unsuccessfully to belittle Jonathan only for him to cast her out, for she had taken the one thing away from him that he desired most: his precious freedom. He knew there was nothing else she could do to ruin him. It gave him some small shred of power over her. A very bittersweet ending some would say, as Everilda had spent many moons tormenting poor Jonathan all for him to say to her, "Get out of here." Well, you could only commend the man for that as it was a brave act indeed.

Whereas now Everilda had nothing left. No strategic moves to play. Jonathan was her only chess piece against Isra and with him refusing to play along, Everilda really needed to get her thinking cap on because surely it was only a matter of time before Isra came crashing in. Everilda mused as she was positioned on the steps almost as if in a daydream. Her eyes changed their focus to the robust cherry tree that dominated the greenery just beyond Wingdom's Academy, staring at the ruby red cherries that were slowly becoming overripe, soon to be rotting. Just like her. Running out of time.

I have to do something. I must get back at her in some form of another, but how can one achieve this? Darn it. I've used everything I could have possibly estimated but Isra is out for blood. She'd have my veins etched onto a frame if she had the means to attain them. So what in the heavens am I going to do, hmm? Everilda said to herself, very much frustrated with how this had turned out.

Nothing was going how she had thought it would. She had exhausted every resource she had in her domain but now she'd have to conjure up something much more fruitful if she was going to stand a chance against Isra.

"Maybe I'll just ask old Magnus for some advice, some useful tidbit that could prove advantageous in defeating her. Perhaps if I show him my reasoning of things and he came around to the version of events as I conceive them to be, maybe dear old Isra will get banished. Torn down. And I won't have to deal with her any longer. Yes, maybe that is my best option."

Everilda conferred with herself although she had said it out loud. Apparently, she had deemed that deceiving the wise old ministries at Wingdom's was the ultimate and let's face it, only method of being victorious.

"Yes, that shall be my grand plan," Everilda smiled as she gave herself a wink.

21

Magnus Wingdom was sitting upright in his lackluster classroom with plain walls as suddenly a loud thump echoed onto his door.

That's peculiar. I have given all my protégés early release, so who could be knocking on my door? Hmm, the professor asked himself as he lifted himself from his wooden chair in preparation to answer it.

However, the door flew open at once and Everilda stood there with a worried expression as Magnus could only look stunned in response.

"And may I ask what brings you here, Everilda?" Magnus queried, almost matching the look of concern that was etched upon her face. However, the renowned faculty member wasn't about to tolerate any hogwash, as he knew Everilda was famous for spouting a tall tale.

Everilda straightened her long midnight-blue cloak, loosening it a tiny bit around her neck so she had room to fully compose her voice as if she was auditioning for some big performance. One would guess that being a pathological liar was just as exhausting as rehearsing for the performance of a lifetime. Everilda pursed her lips but then had to remain mute for a moment to pause. She hadn't quite practiced what she was going to say, not exactly. But that was Everilda all over.

She'd go in feet first, not knowing what big black hole she'd end up in.

"I am afraid it is pertaining to Isra," the witch muttered with a furrowed brow. "You see, of late, she hasn't really been herself and I am sorry for it is my fault, sir," Everilda explained with her eyes facing the floor before she raised them upward to face her highly ordained teacher in an awkward stare.

However, Magnus wasn't reacting in the manner Everilda had expected. She had thought he'd be wholly cross, but instead there was pretty much no reaction at all.

Oh, that can't be right? Everilda questioned herself. *Why isn't he shouting fiery insults of rules and regulations at me? Doesn't he realize what I've just said to him? Oh golly, this is artless to say the least.*

"How so is this laid at your door?" Magnus probed her earnestly.

His eyes glowered over her like rockets that were about to launch, but maintained a steady sense of pause before they went full blast into the ether. It was almost as though he was coaxing Everilda for the full story. Perhaps some would say that the wise old pompous man knew that she was spinning him a line tossed into the fire and harnessed with more toxic lies to boot.

Everilda lowered herself as though to take a bow but then she thought that seemed way too gracious for someone like herself to undertake, so maybe she should just be snappy about it and come out of the garden already, having spent enough time hiding underneath the explicable shadow ferns for much time already.

"I am so deplorable to have to convey to you that Isra and I have had a disagreement of sorts. You see, we both fell for the same bothersome man and although he agreeably had his good points, neither of us could compete over him any longer. I tried to make amends for my part in the whole affair, but Isra failed to see that. If she had taken note of my reasoning, she would have seen that I was in fact trying to sway her from making a mistake that would have been in the greatest magnitude, but she's a stubborn soul. She's gone off in search of malevolent forces with the intent to destroy me," Everilda recited callously.

She was banking on the idea that Magnus would believe her sordid tale with much glee as her sky-blue eyes glossed over him as if she was a saccharine girl in the virtuous chaste society. Which of course, she was not. Oh please, Everilda holy? Do me a favor. It's simply not feasible. The girl had been led astray by so much debauchery in her time that it was impossible for her to retain any goodness.

"Aha, I think I discern your meaning, child, but do inform me why it has taken you so long to appear at my domain with this very crucial and also impregnable matter?" Magnus questioned again. Clearly the old man was not impressed with Everilda's act of delaying his notification to Isra's dimensionality of which she had inevitably turned to acts of malice.

"It has been complex for me, sir," Everilda said in an apologetic voice. "I do foresee that she is on her torrid way to come for my very soul." Everilda came at him quickly for she didn't want to leave anything out of her fictional anecdote that could incite Magnus to believe she wasn't being truthful.

"Don't worry yourself over that," Magnus assured her with a smile. "We at Wingdom's do not tolerate any of our students engaging in the forbidden arts, no matter what the circumstances that led them to undertake such extremities," he added swiftly.

Everilda let out a huge sigh of relief. *Phew, I got away with it. He's soaked it up exactly how I deemed he would. Now Isra is really in for it, big time. Ha, I can't wait to see her face when she is exposed and soon expelled from the academy. She will never cross me again,* Everilda cackled to herself in jubilation.

The snide grin on her face detailed the amusement from her wicked plan. It lingered amongst her breath as though she had just whispered a devilish secret to an innocent child.

And it could have been left there with nothing more said between protégé and the professor, however at exactly the very wrong moment the wooden floor creaked and the door flew open revealing a glowing Isra standing there with a smirk on her face like she had just struck gold. But as for her glow, my goodness! The auroral lime green that beamed from Isra's eyes practically lit up the besmirched classroom.

Magnus was the first to acknowledge Isra as he beamed at her which was bizarre when you think of what Everilda had just informed him of, but there he went starting in a former mannerism.

"Ah Miss Isra, you decided to grace us with your presence. How terribly enlightening of you! Miss Everilda here has been telling tales of your delightful adventures."

There was a pause as Everilda's eyes met Isra's with an unversed stare. It was one that could only spell out the words, "Oh fuck. I am in for it now. She knows!"

"Oh, I bet she has!" was Isra's cold and delayed response. Although like Magnus, Isra had a smile on her that gave the impression that she found Everilda's shifty eye movements rather entertaining.

The fact that someone who was so bold and confident to one-up her was suddenly trembling in her midst. That gave Isra a great wholly sense of efficacy, for she had come here on a very delicate matter that needed resolving.

"Isra," Everilda began in a low voice. "Before you go gallivanting to conclusions, I must try and plead my case."

Everilda attempted to beseech Isra, trying to sound earnest, but it was apparent to all in the room that she was not.

"To hell with your excuses, Everilda. I'm getting quite irritated by them. And now, you and I are going to have a quiet, intimate chat away from prying eyes because we have some unfinished business, wouldn't you agree?" Isra pressed with a sly grin as she instantaneously conjured a bright lime green orb in the palm of her hand. The orb dazzled brilliantly illuminated with shimmering green sparks almost like fireflies that were being incinerated by the most hot tempered of flames.

Isra stood back to admire her handiwork, flashing Everilda an equally snide and sinister grin before retorting back to her foe, "Oh that? It's just magic. It's not enough to obliterate you, of course. But it may well inflict a lot of indeterminable damage while we hang fire.

Discover just what this charming little commodity will do to you! Hang fire? Now isn't that the most perfect term of phrase to describe your dire, dreary fate? Oh girl, you've messed with things much bigger than you and now you are going to pay the piper," Isra remarked, still appearing very much amused by the whole affair.

You'd think that Isra would be even the tiniest bit pissed off but no, she was very much reveling in seeing Everilda almost drop to her knees in incomprehensible fear. However, Everilda was in her thoughts, having them surge around her head like a fireball that had run out of gas. She needed to do something quickly or else the consequences could be fatal indeed.

Everilda closed her eyes as if in deep concentration, a gesture that seemed to amuse both Isra and Magnus who seemingly was on the side of Isra. But to be honest, the wise old professor was likely neutral on both ends. Or he'd be on the side of whoever was more dormant as far as the light was concerned.

Everilda whispered something into the atmosphere as though incanting an illicit chant she had feasted upon once when she had paid attention to one of her lessons. The fair-haired witch was slowly reciting something that was barely audible. All anyone heard was, "Wisssi woo. Wooo. Roooon." It sounded as if she was speaking in another dialect and clearly had no comprehension of what she was enacting although she did her utmost to remain in deep concentration. Not that Everilda had ever got that notion, of course.

Within an instant, a glowing surge of yellow gold light flew across the murky classroom, giving it a fresh sheen of paint in the sense that suddenly everything was visible in full blown color. You could see the antique desks, the basic yet sturdy wooden chairs and even the ceiling. It had never been this bright in here, but Everilda's magic was making it reborn anew. The sinister force of golden energy danced around the room like a rocket until it settled on its target: Isra.

Only the pompous Magnus stepped in! The bold man took a brave step and pushed Isra away with his right hand, sending her flying across his desk in a flurry. The startled witch landed on the ground in a heap, clearly bemused and slightly dizzy as whiteness encompassed her vision. Isra's world became a blur as she tried her utmost to zone in on what was occurring between Magnus and Everilda, but to no avail as she was lost in her own nauseous daze.

The golden light hit Magnus in a nanosecond, realizing that this was its destination. Sizzling and burning brighter, it gathered its malevolence, blinding all occupants of the room with its heightened magic before it stopped and the majestic Magnus totally vanished. In his place, a brown earthworm wriggled along the cold stone floor.

Isra, who was still slightly off balance from Magnus sending her onto the floor in a crash, regained her footing, standing up although she still felt tremendously dizzy from the experience. Isra bent down to inspect the unsuspecting creature that was now in her hand, picking Magnus the worm up and cradling him carefully before sitting him on his desk.

Although as she did so, she almost dropped him as he suddenly boomed in her ear, "What in the hell has happened to me? I've never once been transformed by one of my students in all my years. Goodness gracious. Get me out of here and into my well-bodied form," he snapped in a tiresome squeaky voice.

"Good question," Isra remarked, eyeing Everilda with a vicious grin. The satisfaction that displayed across her face was inexplicable as she glowered over her foe with careful fervor.

Isra strode right up to Everilda with a snide grin. It was surely one that displayed both hatred and pleasure as she chuckled callously, looking back at Magnus and then focusing her attention back to Everilda once more as she remarked, "I never imagined in all my tenure that I would witness such a feat of stupidity. It pains me to say it, but I knew you were dense, Everilda. Of course, I had never foreseen something as disastrous as this. Girl, what the hell were you even thinking of?" Isra probed Everilda in a bold voice.

"In fact, dear girl, don't even bother acknowledging that with an answer. I know the real you. I know exactly what goes on up in that pea sized brain of yours. It took me a while to comprehend the ins and outs, but now I've finally got it. For so long I had been weeping and blaming myself for the transgressions that occurred between us, but now I know. It's not me. It was never me. All along, all the drama and debacles. It was all you, Everilda. There was always just something amiss with you and I can't believe it took me so many weeks to fathom it. To dissect it for what it truly is. Even Jonathan was just a victim in your wake, despite how much he did to me," Isra uttered with confidence.

"Of course, this little error of yours is likely to cost you in the most unfavorable manner but let me affirm to you this. I'd love to give you what is rightfully yours. The delectably sweet revenge that I have been craving for many moons now, however I shall refrain from that."

Isra continued, allowing a small pause to drift amongst all the silence that beckoned as Everilda was for once mute. "Because I've realized a little tidbit that I failed to comprehend before. I could kill you. I could tear you down right where you stand now and take delight in your pathetic defeat, but I won't. Why? You'll be in misery for eons after this nonsensical act, Everilda. Banished and cast out, rendered useless to the world. The exact same fate you attempted to bestow upon my person. I won't need to do anything to you. You'll spend long, tiresome centuries being reminded of how you failed to vaporize me. People will howl with laughter over your tragic tale, sweetheart. And so I will not exterminate you as I could, because your greatest pain will be to live with that humiliation for years to come."

Isra looked back at Magnus for a second as the worm reared his head eagerly as if he was in agreement over what she was saying before taking her eyes off the brown ochre-colored sniveling distraction.

"It's not about me seeking revenge any longer. The fact you'll be overshadowed by this for eternity is enough to satisfy my soul. I'll be reveling in this until the day I perish. If such a day ever comes," Isra added callously with an afterthought.

Isra had actually forgotten she now possessed magics way beyond her understanding and perhaps there was now a very resourceful use for them since she had well and truly done what she had come here to do. Belittling Everilda was the very last thing on her list and as far as Isra was concerned, she was done here. There was nothing more to say between her and her weakened foe, though she'd had a most riveting day, to say the least. It was beautifully dramatic in every sense of the word.

Everilda still remained silent, for what more was there to say? She'd tried to conquer Isra. Everilda had done her utmost to convince the bigwig of Wingdom's that Isra was forsaken, tainted with the most devilish magics. And it was true; Isra was, but Isra had one-upped Everilda because of one stupid, dumb mistake the amateurish fair-haired witch had tried to enact against Isra.

I suppose you could say the lesson here for Everilda was do not rush into the fire haphazardly without having a full embodiment of just what you were crashing into, just in case you got seared by the flames. Everilda wasn't even that proficient in magics beyond basic incantations, so really it was no surprise that she made quite the discombobulation, but as it turned out her embarrassment was far from over as a gray owl with long, silvery gray wings materialized out of nowhere into the chaos.

The owl whose bewildering blue eyes wandered over to Magnus and examined his predicament before whispering a few choice words that none of the participants including Magnus himself were able to hear. Immediately upon these words being uttered, a white light with a golden sheen circulated around Magnus's worm form, getting brighter as it completely saturated him before he was restored in a flash looking quite irritated at none other than Everilda.

"Miss Everilda, where do I even start with your discrepancies?" Magnus bellowed, still adjusting to being back in his humanized form. The petulant man shook some dust away from him as it lingered on his formal attire.

"I…" Everilda began in a hushed voice, unable to properly speak for some peculiar reason of which she did not know.

"SILENCE!" Magnus roared at her. He was absolutely seething with rage. Magnus's eyes were glowing bright red. That was how angry he was with her.

"Everilda Daughtry, I first of all banish you from the Wingdom's

Academy never to return under any circumstance for as long as you live," Magnus shouted as Everilda's face only resembled shame and perilous fear.

Everilda was pretty much trembling in every sense of the word. Her hands shook by her sides as she stood awaiting the next installment of her fate. Whereas Isra on the other hand was very much calm and controlled, almost relaxed as she stood on the sidelines as an onlooker witness to such a well conducted reprimand. It was far more than she could ever have delivered. And Isra had to admit she was gloating quite a bit because this was really an enjoyable show that had exceeded her expectations.

Oh, just keep it coming. This is far too rapturous for me to even describe, Isra thought to herself as she too lay in wait for whatever came next for the painfully and so massively torn down Everilda.

"It incites me to think of what delectably entrancing delights are coming next! Oh, deary me, I shouldn't have said that! Oh well!" Isra burst out laughing a little too loudly much to the contempt of every other faculty member who was in on the proceedings.

"Miss Isra. I thank you for your time today, but I'd prefer it if you made off with yourself now," Magnus instructed Isra in a stern voice.

Obviously, he didn't want Isra to witness anymore of the cruel fate that was becoming of Everilda, much to Isra's dismay as she was thoroughly enjoying this.

Isra acknowledged Magnus's request by retreating from where she was standing at the side of the classroom before making a low bow proceeding to make her exit as she made her way toward the door, but Magnus was way ahead of Isra, waving his hand in the air to halt her departure.

"Hang on, Miss Isra," Magnus commanded her in a low voice. "I presume you will want to be a witness for the following dissemination."

Magnus's words forced the amused Isra to turn her head around, awaiting whatever was coming as she stood patiently waiting by the door. Just what fanciful things were in store she had no inclination of, but whatever it was, Magnus had deemed she was worthy of hearing it. And in Isra's mind, that meant something indeed.

"Oh?" Isra questioned with a slightly mystified glance. "Well, if you insist, I shall of course delay my leave just to see this with my own eyes." She sniggered, resisting the temptation to lick her lips. Oh, Everilda was in for it, this time, well and truly bit the banger but it was rather satisfying for Isra so she just kept her mouth shut as the show began to unfold.

"Miss Everilda," Magnus began once more. This time his tone was a little more decorum in nature as he too appeared to be enjoying this.

Well, that's new, Isra marveled to herself in thought. Again, with a snide grin plastered on her face that was impossible to conceal.

"You are banished from Wingdom's Academy as by my direct order, but not only that, child..." A pause lingered in the room as every soul in the room stood in anticipation just able to bear the suspense of what was next. "But dear girl, I, Magnus Wingdom strip you of any esoteric power despite any virtues or skills you may have honed for yourself, until the very day when your ceases. Hereby ordained in witness of Sir Otto Jinx, secondary in charge to myself. You are dismissed."

"But... I ... But..." Everilda stammered, unable to comprehend what just happened. The tears pummeled down her usually rosy, red cheeks rendering her almost unrecognizable with the salty saline fluid dripping down her face. Those once glossy sapphire blue eyes now puffy and red from where she had excreted so much melancholy.

"SILENCE!" Magnus raised his left hand as if he was preparing to battle a torturous, vile beast and all Everilda could do was close her eyes as her fate was unmercifully bestowed to her.

22

The rain began to pelt down in a torrential shower much to the dismay of Everilda who was now mortal and alone, wandering alone in the woods seeking shelter. Having been banished from Wingdom's, she was now homeless as well as losing her greatest asset she'd ever laid claim to. Her magic.

But it was gone. Stolen from her without a care and now she'd have to go about the rest of her days miserable, bitter, and desolate. What a culture shock for someone who was so obsessed with having control over another being to now having that tainted ability ripped away from her.

The good folk at Wingdom's had done their utmost showing no sympathy to Everilda's plight, for not only was she banished but she was now mortal, too, a horrific cross she'd likely have to bear for the rest of her untimely eternity. Of course, Everilda was always going to bounce back. She had an ace up her sleeve. There was more than one way to skin a cat, but she had actually forgotten how she'd dealt with these kinds of situations without having great magnitude over another person.

"Hmm, there must have been a way once upon a time where I got one over on somebody without the dark arts," Everilda mused to herself as she trampled through the soaking wet fern-green grass.

She was on her way to poor old Jonathan's humble abode. Not being content with all the mental anguish she had put him through, Everilda was going to relight the fire in the callous man's heart, just without the magic this time.

Unbeknownst to Everilda however, she wasn't alone in this desolate terrain.

Isra drew her long midnight blue cloak up to her head, wistfully feeling the icy chill in the air. Raindrops splattered onto her form like electricity as Isra looked up at her foe with a wicked smile.

The energy pulsated from within her. Isra felt entranced yet at peace with the mesmerizing power that was within her. The callous magnificence had locked itself into her soul keeping it barricaded from anything that was untainted as though it was a fortitude of uncertainty.

Isra scanned the area closely for any signs of life other than herself and Everilda, already having stalked the former witch for almost an hour. She'd kept a watchful eye on her arch nemesis, not taking her attention away from Everilda for a second, for it could all go horribly wrong. Or, that would be the outcome that Everilda would be likely hoping for.

Nope, nothing. Not a soul out there. Just rain tearing down upon our lands cursing it with its moist damp cloudy furor. Isra conversed with herself in a mind bubble, planning out exactly how she'd maneuver herself because of course even in the harshest weathers, one would still have to be incredibly strategic.

Everilda was totally unaware of Isra's propinquity, something Isra would revel in as she wanted to swoop in and catch Everilda just when she wasn't expecting it. Everilda seemed to be heading a little way off the border of Seclera as she continued to pummel the ground with her sodden wet feet. Interesting, as the weary Everilda seemed to be heading toward the direction of Jonathan's cottage that was not too far away from the main border that guarded Seclera and Spirisity.

Oh, how very sweet! Isra mocked to herself with a spiteful lick of her tongue. *How convenient for her. She loses her powers and the first one she goes crawling to is him! Ha! What an obsolescent fool he is.*

However, Isra was cut short when she felt the rain patter even harder down onto her head, signaling a storm was brewing as she could feel it in the air. Something was just so destructive about tonight. You could feel it surging through the atmosphere. The most vile and treacherous energies were about to come tumbling down.

"Well, that is most unfortunate, but rain doesn't really bother me," Isra remarked casually to herself as she lifted her cloak from her head. If she was going to get soaked, no amount of rich velvet would protect her from the rough climate.

Isra decided that she would follow Everilda for a little while just to see where the fateful witch, or should we say mortal, was heading. After all, it was likely Everilda would lead Isra straight to Jonathan.

Now that would be something because Isra had come out here to deal with Everilda. She had forgotten to include measly Jonathan into the bargain, so having two birds and just one stone to kill them with would really be a delight.

Isra perched herself outside Jonathan's cottage. She was drenched. Her hair was lying flat against her back, completely matted with how wet it was, but Isra was being clever. She wasn't outside the front of his cottage but merely sheltering herself around the corner, in the exact same place a certain raven had been not so long ago. Isra had expected Everilda to arrive at any moment but so far there was no sign of Everilda or Jonathan for that matter.

Hmmm, that is most peculiar, Isra thought to herself in wonder.

She was most curious as to how she might have missed them when she had been so stead worthy in arranging herself in the most sophisticated position as to catch them both unawares like a deadly snake lying in the grass ready to strike. Isra was far more cunning than a reptilian species, having the ability to hone in on any place and make herself blend in like a chameleon, of course without the gift of being able to change her coloring. Although that would likely be frightfully thrilling for the young witch if she could master such a skill.

"They must be around here somewhere. But where?" Isra uttered out loud, being exceptionally careful not to be overheard for she knew eyes and ears were all over the place. "Perhaps they have outwitted me. I must have discarded a very important detail, for they are not here. I'd suspected they'd have nowhere to go but this desolate vagabond of a home," Isra recited in a slightly defeated voice. Clearly, she was annoyed that Jonathan and Everilda were not here to face the music and most importantly, herself.

But just as Isra peered beyond the corner, just a little way down the grassy bank, what did she catch sight of? Oh, it wasn't, was it? Yes. None other than Jonathan and Everilda were skin to skin almost embracing as their bodies were firmly pressed together in the wet and windy downpour.

"Oh no, it can't be. What in the devil?" Isra cursed, almost revealing herself from her graceful hiding place as she felt a pang in her heart.

She'd done her utmost to stalk Everilda and Jonathan, but now she was wishing she hadn't. The pain inside her still beating heart was far too much to bear. It was stinging in her chest, practically turning inside out as it unraveled inside Isra's fragile body.

"Oh to hell with this! I cannot take it anymore!" Isra screamed out, wailing her frustration unto anyone or anything that would listen.

She looked over at Everilda and Jonathan again. Seemingly they were very close knitted for two people that considered each other to be mortal enemies. Ha, you'd really have to excuse the expression because Everilda was just that.

If Isra hadn't been so consumed with rage and anger, she might have wondered whether Jonathan had knowledge of Everilda's unceremonious dissolution as far as her powers stood. However, Isra was in no mood for curiosity in any form. She'd had it, literally.

There was no more time for games. This was it. The grand repertoire.

And with a slight wave of her hand just in time to catch the adolescent tears streaming down her cheek, Isra dissipated into thin air.

23

Lightning cascaded across the darkened midnight blue sky. The coloring was more black than blue in nature as you could only just see the emblem of the glowing white full moon shimmering amongst the density of it all.

Isra hadn't even recognized it was a full moon having been way too busy, moping around. Her heart was abreast of revenge and nothing but. What was left of her mind was cluttered and scrutinized with a fine-tooth comb as she'd been analyzing every last segment of the Jonathan and Everilda drama. Not even realizing she was neglecting parts of herself, she flurried around in a hurry anxious to have all of this over and done with.

Now standing on the very same mountain peak where she had tasted that first sweet bite of dark fervor, Isra glanced up at the moon and admired its beauty, for even in the darkest of nights it still shone the brightest. But light wasn't something she was going to fully acknowledge at this point in time. Isra had come here to finally release herself from this abhorrent disguise and the horrific pain that resided in her heart that she was at last going to find salvation from, as well as to save herself from the bitter doom that was crushing every last fragment of her and could bear no longer.

It was no surprise that with the dark foreboding atmosphere a shrieking flash of yellow gold lightning dominated the skies, adding a golden glow to the almost black hell that surged from above. The harsh crackling of the lightning distracted Isra for a moment as the warm yellow light brought a gleaming fiery flare onto herself almost as though she was covered in flames, but then it flew back over, sending another loud hammering as it merged with the thunder that raged across the land with severe fortitude.

If it wasn't for the bitter coldness of her heart, she'd likely have become shell shocked with the icy cold of the rain that towered down upon her, hammering down onto her slender form and drenching her yet again in its cleansing torrent.

But none of that mattered. Another lightning rod sparked across the fiery blackened skies almost missing the moon by an inch. Isra didn't hold back any longer. Reaching down past her neck and letting her hand linger above her chest for a second, she almost stopped in pause.

If I do this now, this will be everything. There will be no turning back. I will be the very thing that I have never wanted to be, she said to herself in bemused thought with the temptation only becoming more tantalizing.

Another few seconds passed as Isra finally reached into her chest. The sensation in her body was almost indescribable as her hand fumbled around inside her ribcage searching for the one organ that would bring her salvation. Her heart. Latching a firm grip onto the dried-out organ, Isra fought back the deluge of pain that dragging it out from inside her body caused. She jerked it out of her chest with one swift tug, taken aback as it sat in the palm of her hand saturated in her warm, salty, ruby red blood.

"I cannot bear this any longer. Darkness, take me. Fear, release me. I swear on all that is unjust that I will be your loyal savior for as long as my life deems it!" Isra announced in a sharp cry to the land holding her battered, broken heart up for offering up to the sky in an exchange.

Once more with feeling, holding the precious entity in her palm,

Isra raised her hand upward to the skies. A triumphant act of defiance indeed, she focused her attention on the heart which all of a sudden miraculously transformed from red to black. Holding the blackened heart, Isra breathed a sigh of relief.

"RELEASE ME. DARKNESS, I AM YOURS!" Isra shouted out, holding the torn entity still in her hand. "I surrender to your power. And with this worthless gift in return, please accept my humble token of affections. And with this kiss, I am eternally giving myself to you."

She cried out once more as lightning tore down upon her, surrounding her in the most efflorescent golden shards of light as someone faithfully heard her call. To conclude the ritual she had dutifully performed, Isra, still soaking wet and holding her blackened and bruised heart, blew a kiss up to the sky as though to give something back in return for whatever she may now be blessed or cursed with.

As the white lightning that was now clashing across the darkened skies showed no sign of simmering down, a muffled sound could be heard from the nearby crevice of the mountain peak although the sobriety wasn't about to cease. The rain continued to hurl down onto this shadowy land as though it was healing everything after that ghastly dark feat that Isra had unleashed from within herself.

From his safe spot above the crevice, Astrid the raven unfurled his feathers, shaking off a few stray rain drops. He shuddered while displaying a furrowed brow, giving a look of sheer concern.

Astrid had witnessed Isra rip out her heart, giving it up to the darkness. He had seen it all with his beady eyes.

***To be continued in *Kissing Darkness*. ***

INTRODUCING KISSING DARKNESS
DARK SPELL SERIES BOOK 2

Samuel rushed into his office clutching a now lukewarm mug of coffee in his left hand. The man had already been experiencing a chaotic morning, having the metaphysical chimes practically ringing in his ears from the "on high," but the light bringer was exhausted. Just imagine his surprise, thinking he was alone when he was met by the solemn glance of Astrid.

"Ah boy, I wondered where you were. Do you like slightly warm coffee? I can't say I recommend it too highly," Samuel chirped grimacing as he took a sip.

"I'm not here for the sanctimonious refreshments, Samuel," Astrid countered, clearly looking pissed at Samuel, but why he was upset Samuel had no inclination of. Could it be that the dear friend of Astrid had offended the poor raven, or did he have his feathers in a twist over something? Or perhaps someone. A certain feminine he was rather fond of? Well, it could be that.

"Yes, well, I'd rather have a fresh one but there's just no time, you know? So much to do," Samuel countered, swigging the rest of the coffee that was now stone cold. "That is vile indeed," the light bringer sputtered, pulling a face of disgust as he looked upon the raven favorably.

"So do tell me. What brings you here in such a dander, hmm? It's not your time of the month, is it?" Samuel asked Astrid, noting the raven was situated a little farther than usual today.

How strange. He's normally so chatty. I normally cannot get the bastard to shut up actually, Samuel motioned to himself in thought as he realized Astrid's temperament was very different this morning. Slightly brasher than usual.

"Actually, I've just come back from witnessing Isra give up her heart to darkness," Astrid replied, clearly not beating around the bush. His tone was icy but yet pungent as if was surrounded by ferocious flames that were not about to cease any time soon.

"Oh. That," Samuel murmured. "Do tell me, what is going on? I'm afraid I'm a little out of the loop."

Astrid resisted the urge to throw out a sarcastic comeback, having already been told to steer clear of Isra more times than he cared to count. But Samuel was clearly unaware and wasn't about to discipline the raven for filling in the blanks, or at least that was how Astrid hoped it would be.

Never mind, he knows nothing. I'm the guy who gets told in no uncertain terms to get out of there and yet they don't know a damn thing. Utterly ridiculous, Astrid thought quietly to himself, regarding how the "on high" was dealing with the intrepid situation.

"Isra and her foe Everilda are at war with each other," Astrid began in a stern tone. "I have witnessed it for myself. Isra is vengeful and out for blood whereas her opponent—" Astrid stopped mid-speech for fear that whatever he said now would get him into a lot of hot water. After all, he wasn't supposed to be within claws distance of the witch.

But evidently, Samuel had no clue of what was occurring, so better to say now than later, right? What's the worst that could emerge from such a thing? Astrid doubted not much as he'd already caught sight of enough tormenting things already.

"Everilda," Astrid continued, "was a witch, but now is mortal thanks to the gracious folk over at Wingdom's who saw to it."

Samuel almost spat in horrendous shock. "You have to be joking surely? You mean to tell me that our witch has a foe that is now mortal? Ordained by the very academy we've had our eyes on for months? Where the fuck is James?" Samuel countered in frustration, banging his fists upon his desk.

"Oh no, this is too much for a morning. I need a shot of whisky. I can't handle it," Samuel snapped, reaching for his decanter eagerly. "And why did the 'on high' not tell us?" Samuel quizzed the raven with a forewarning glance.

"That I do not know. But it's sure to get a lot messier from here on out," Astrid predicted in a somber tone.

"Touché. I must get in touch with James immediately. Someone needs to go down there. Assuming she's still out there causing all manner of havoc," Samuel muttered, almost cursing to himself as he should have been on the ball. He should have been the first to intervene the very second that Isra switched from light to dark.

I should have fucking been there. I've been following this woman since we first heard about her existence. That energy that was surging through her, sending ripples across the earth as she walked in desolate desperation ... I've been reprimanding Astrid for being within arm's length of her and here she turns the tide and I'm not even in the vicinity to do something about it? Oh, I'm an absolute fool, Samuel clashed back and forth with himself in unison.

"Why James?" Astrid asked in a low voice although there was some kind of irritation that Samuel detected in Astrid's tone.

You could tell that Astrid really resented James in some form or another. The way he spoke regarding James was callous as though he'd rather James wasn't there because the way Astrid saw it, James was treading upon his carefully raked soil.

Astrid did not feel very appeased to that.

He'd already threatened to peck James' eyeballs out once, and perhaps if there wasn't some moral justification from Samuel as a result of taking such extremities, then maybe Astrid would have by now. But no, he'd have to sit there and tolerate this human, or whatever James was being involved with as much as Astrid disliked him.

"Because James has experience with witches," Samuel reluctantly comes back to Astrid. "He has the know-how and forward planning on how to deal with them in an efficient manner," Samuel continued in a formal tone.

"How lovely for him. What a novel way to go about your merry life by dealing with witches, as you so ambivalently put it," Astrid scoffed in a sarcastic yet stroppy voice.

Yet again the raven was indicating he was far from happy to hear of James's involvement with the mission at hand, even though Astrid had no physical ability to intervene in regard to Isra.

"Don't start, boy," Samuel chided to the raven with a harsh burning stare, having listened to much of Astrid's ranting already.

"The 'on high' has been communicating to me most of the morning. It's gotten pretty rough down there. Perhaps someone should go down personally and intersect with Isra, as apparently things are messy," Samuel commented with a furrowed brow.

"Oh and let me guess, that someone is James?" Astrid snipped back.

He started to preen his feathers, busying himself with that task and almost ignoring Samuel in a sense. It was as though Astrid felt like something vile had tainted his soft silky black feathers and he was frantically trying to remove it. Or perhaps he was just being an ignorant bastard as he suspected Samuel would answer him with, "Yes."

"No," Samuel responded with a sharp tone.

He veered in closer to the raven, lifting him onto his shoulder so he could speak to him more intently and actually look into Astrid's eyes. This was really the personal touch in Samuel's eyes, the course of action to get the raven to listen to him for a change.

"You really have no comprehension of what's kicked off, do you? I've heard from my wise associates that Isra hasn't just given up her heart to the dark. No. She's done a bit more than that. I mean, if you had been around her since this morning, you'd have known for yourself just what she has unleashed unto our world," Samuel retorted in a serious yet withdrawn voice.

The light bringer was extremely tired and it had already been a rough start to the day. He had a feeling it was about to go worse.

Astrid relented, only giving his master Samuel a sympathetic look. Samuel was rather invested in this mission to tease Isra away from the darkness, after all. He didn't look well thinking about it. Samuel looked pale and lifeless in the face. His normal sky-blue eyes that closely resembled the ocean were lackluster and puffy. All that coffee had not helped Samuel claim some finesse back from his nonexistent sleep.

Clearly there was more to this mission, this fight against the dark, shadowy realms that Samuel was not letting on to. Something that could only be so deeply painful to make him so embroiled in the life of one witch fated for something much more gratifying than anyone could have conjured up for her.

However, Samuel was not surrendering. He would prevail because this was a lifelong devotion. It was fickle for anyone, even Astrid, to think that one set back would cause such a domino effect that would make him give up on a cause he truly believed in. No, Samuel was made of far stronger stuff than to just give in at the first hurdle.

He'd play along with Isra, doing things her way if he had to in order to get her to see the real reasoning of things. If he'd have to, he'd play dirty too. Because Samuel was no stranger to wicked trickery, especially if it meant he'd overcome the demons by cavorting with them just to make them think they had succeeded in bringing damnation.

Astrid was startled as all of sudden with a glint in his blue eyes, Samuel shifted Astrid off of his shoulder with a concerned look placated upon himself.

"I suppose if there is to be any positive resolution in this, I will have to take this matter into my own hands."

The light bringer spoke with a wink, clicking his fingers together as if he had just come up with the plan of a lifetime. That smile that was just about visible signified that Samuel would indeed find a way.

DARK SPELL SERIES READING ORDER

1. Her Dark Love
2. Kissing Darkness
3. Seducing Darkness
4. Queen of Darkness
5. Her Dark Soul
6. Her Dark Heart
7. Her Dark Rose
8. Darkness Reborn

ABOUT THE AUTHOR

USA Today Best Seller Isra Sravenheart resides in the UK. She is an avid reader, particularly in the fantasy and paranormal genres, and very much into all things fairytale and dark in nature. She is also a witty wordsmith.

Isra is known for being obsessed with coffee and very particular towards cats of which she owns four of the buggers.

You can follow Isra through her blog, or any of these social media platforms:

ALSO BY ISRA SRAVENHEART

The Dark Spell Series: Books 1 through 8

Wickedly Good Souls Series: Books 1 through 5

Forbidden Rendezvous With The Devil: Dark Lore Vampire Conspiracies
Book 1

Heart of Oz

Tainted Siren

The Divine Spiritual Truth: A Twinflame Romance